To two of the most important women in my life.

Mom, for always having my back,

And The Sophie,

For always having my future

A Tangled Web

By John G. Walker

Acknowledgements and Dedication

Hello again, everyone. Nice to see you all, and welcome back the Statford Chronicles. I've spent a lot of time here, as have all of you, and I have to tell you: I wasn't expecting to get this far. At this point, I've written over 250,000 words in the Chronicles, and it doesn't look to end anytime soon. There's a lot left to tell about this world, and thanks to some amazing, wonderful, and awesome people, it will keep going.

This wasn't an easy book to write, especially after the last one. Like I said last time, there is a plan. It's not the best plan, at least if your name is Thomas Statford, but it is a good plan for everyone else. I know the plan, and please rest assured, there is a reason for all this happening.

And now, to the people who are part of my life, and make all this possible.

First and foremost, I want to thank my mom, who has always stood by me even when I was a stupid kid who didn't know any better but thought I did. Thank you for being the one who taught me that anything worth having is worth working for.

My heart goes to my niece, The Sophie. She is the inspiration for the brightness in my life, and the one who keeps the old curmudgeonly cynic at bay. You have done well, my young apprentice. I am forever grateful.

As always, to my sister, my brother-in-law, and my grandmother, you are the facets of the jewel that is this family. I thank you for not giving up on me; that means more to me than you will ever know.

Erika Pryor, my editor… The words here would not be right if not for you. You gave me constant, unending hell for every wrong word choice, and I deserved it. Thank you for keeping me on the straight and narrow.

The cover wrapped around this book is by the wonderfully talented Starla Huchton, a fantastic author in her own right and, as you can see, a visual genius. You keep me trying to make the stories worth having your amazing covers. Go look at her work at www.designedbystarla.com. Do it now!

The RoTaNoWriMo crew... Gods... What can be said that doesn't violate every bit of ethics and decency in the free world and likely get me deported? How about the fact that without the support from all of you, I would have quit before the first words of the Chronicles were written? That especially goes for our Fearless Leader, The Dreamhand, Dave Robison. Go check out the Roundtable Podcast at www.roundtablepodcast.com, as it's one of the most informative writer podcasts on the interwebs. A thousand thanks is not enough.

And as always, to You, faithful readers, who took a chance on a tale about a private detective with a fantastical bent and kept on reading: Thank you. When I say that you complete me, I mean it. You are wonderful and if you keep reading, I'll keep writing.

Stick around for a fun little announcement at the end.

Now, back to the world of the Statford Chronicles, where things are not what they seem, and the world just got so much more complicated for poor Tom. See you on the other side.

-jgw

Chapter One

My blood went cold as I whipped my head around in a momentary panic at a whisper. Whether it was real or imagined, I could not know; more likely it was just a trick from the howl of the wind through the cracks riddling the drafty place I knew as my prison. Those moments of panic came more and more often. The flickering of the cheap florescent bulbs above me were an epileptic's nightmare. The flashes were accompanied by an annoying buzz, you know that dead hum, a fly that stays just in your ear and just out of reach from your hand. All I could do was stare at them for hours, even after my head would ache to splitting. After a bit, I'd break the monotony by looking elsewhere. Each glance gave me something new to marvel over. A crack in a tile above me, a scratch on the metal door showing gouged out paint, a misalignment in the floor tiles beneath me; the stale stink of the air, drowning me. There was an oppression to the place that infected my every pore, and every sense seemed to suffer for it.

From where I sat, the aluminum chair separating my ass from the frigid floor, seemed to shudder with my every breath. I felt almost buoyant, even with the idea I could be spilled unceremoniously to the floor at any moment. While I floated there, I kept finding something else to ponder, anything besides my aching skull. My head pounded from whatever pharmaceutical cocktail they had given me, and my mouth felt like someone had scrubbed it out with an old gym sock from 1972, a good year but not my taste. Something inside told me that I had been through worse; a lot worse.

There was a mirror bolted into the wall of my bathroom, which I found was just highly polished metal. That was likely in case I decided to try taking over the facility with a few shards of glass. Of course I wasn't that stupid; plans that ridiculous only worked in bad movies and television shows.

I had looked closely in the metal, gazing in shock at the stranger staring back at me. There was a brown stubble on my head, like I had just been shorn for boot camp. My face was shaved clean, revealing a jawline that looked strong. There were scars on my face, remnants of possible fights I might have won or lost, even though the outcome didn't matter. A particularly deep one ran down my right cheek. Dark brown eyes, innocent of any knowledge, or even any real life, looked back at me. I did not know that face, or anything about the man it belonged to.

Did I?

I checked out the only window in the room, a pathetic thing maybe eighteen inches to a side. A rabbit or a small child might have been able to get through it, but I didn't have a prayer. A combination of wrought iron bars and an iron mesh covered the milky glass, making the portal to the outside almost useless, but allowing some natural light to pass through on to me. The snow outside was still falling, thick and fluffy, as it had since I arrived, even though I could not tell when I first got there.

Staring at the paper in front of me, I twirled the pen in my fingers. That I was given the luxury of a pen was shocking since I was considered a danger and menace to society. I had schmoozed the doctor enough to allow me the writing instrument, practically begging for it so I could write the one person I thought would understand what was going on. The doctor also thought it would be a great idea to try and get my thoughts on paper so I would understand myself better.

I had a grandiose plan, one I thought was foolproof. It failed miserably. Because my memory had more gaps in it than the smiles of the average first grade class, the more I tried to force everything and anything from my past, the more holes appeared. I could barely remember past the prior week. Anything that might have been in what passed for my brain that seemed older than seven days I would jot down so to possibly jog my memory about unknown places and things. Hopefully, it would start an avalanche in my mind to tell me exactly what the hell happened to me and how the hell I ended up in a mental institution, wearing blue sweatpants and a matching sweatshirt, and sitting at a table wondering what was real and what were the fantastical ravings of a madman. What made it worse? I was that madman, or so they said.

So far, the farthest I had gotten was my name on an envelope: Tom Statford.

The name was right; the doctor called me Tom, and I saw that name in my chart whenever I could glance at it. I didn't know my name when I woke up in the chair the last time, and learning my name was the first in a great many surprises.

I found myself doodling on the paper, symbols that meant nothing and everything to me. A quartered circle. A crucifix over a dollar sign. A Chinese ideogram. A featureless doll. A feather. Meaningless and meaningful in my mind, they and a dozen others chased each other around the paper, bringing whispers of memories. There was fire, and blood, and pain.

So much pain.

The voice in my head spoke up then, telling me things I could scarcely believe. I unconsciously put the words on paper, my hand moving of its own accord. The pen formed dark marks on the white sheet, my own ideas and ghosts of ideas, describing things going from the mundane to the fantastic and back with mind-numbing speed.

I had a mother, so I wrote the letter to her. According to the doctor, I had killed a man in one of the coldest ways possible: execution style with a bullet to the brainpan. That wasn't why I was in the Twin Friezes Institute for Mental Health. I was in the loony bin because I believed in gods, and the gods had told me to do it.

Not just one God, mind you, but multiple pantheons of them. Stuff out of legends and movies and comic books were real to me, and I was their chosen emissary, the one who kept bad things from happening between deities and mortals. They all really existed, and they chose me to keep things kosher.

Yeah, I know. Written down, it does sound like something out of the mouth and mind of a lunatic or a sci-fi writer trying to make a buck. Welcome to what passed for my life, at least in my head. When I was told what I did, though, it almost made me wish I could forget everything all over again.

When I first woke up in the Chair, my nerves singing from both chemicals and the aftermath of an electroshock, I remembered nothing. Not my name, my birthday, my family, nothing. All I knew was pain, the kind of white-hot pain that tears the soul as it rips through the flesh, leaving nothing but smoldering ruin behind. Seeing the doctor brought rage, even though I didn't have a clue who he was past the white coat he wore. I took a swing at him, which made him do the smart thing and put artificial sleep in my veins.

If some of this is rambling and makes no real sense, I'm sorry. I'm still learning it as I go along. It's not a fun experience, not knowing who you are outside of what someone tells you, or you've thrown your life away for a dream that never actually existed. Or that the foggy memories in your pounding skull were the delusions of grandeur belonging to a murderous psycho. That last probability hurt the worst.

So there I sat, trying to focus on the past to get a sense of my present. My mind drifted to the doctor again, and anger, not the rage I usually felt, sprang up. The mellowing was either my growing acceptance of the situation, or the huge amounts of phenobarbital coursing through my system thanks to Jaime, the gargantuan orderly who held me down so it could be injected.

Of course, I was thinking it was more the latter. Something told me Tom Statford was not a "mellow" guy.

More doodles formed on the page, this time meaningless because of tears forming in my eyes. I had no idea what they were. Names? Dates? Hell, it could have been the Pythagorean Theorem for I knew, but it seemed as if it should be important, like it should mean something more than a bunch of useless scribbles. I tried to focus on the writing but the harder I looked, the more blurry it got.. Wiping my tears away with one hand did nothing so I put the pen down to use both hands to clear my eyes.

I covered my eyes with both hands and got blessed darkness. Pushing my palms against my eyelids got starbursts and a slight bit of pain. I latched on to that pain, since it was the only thing that felt real to me, it was truly mine; I could clearly remember it had happened to me because I had done it to myself. The pain wasn't something I was told happened, but something that I witnessed and experienced. Paradoxically, it felt good, even if it caused a few more tears to squeeze out. I took several deep breaths to try and center myself. That wasn't something the doctor had taught me, so I assumed it was a learned thing from my life before the prison my mind had become, and this place that kept my body under lock and key. There had to be a before, since I could not have been born in such a place, especially with the laundry list of horrible things I was being of accused of.

My hands fell to the table, involuntarily crinkling the papers with the gesture. I felt my throat constrict from emotions I was barely keeping in check. There was something murmuring in the echoes like a breeze through tall grass, somewhere in the back of my memory, and it was saying a word. Try as I might, I could not understand it, even though I felt in my soul I should. It was like a song from childhood, but considering I couldn't even remember the week prior, I shouldn't have been surprised that I couldn't bring it to the forefront of what was supposed to be my brain.

I opened my eyes and looked at the papers. The tears on my hands had smudged the ink into meaningless blobs, bringing forth rage. I tore the pages apart, shredding some of them to confetti. My words of madness fluttered all over the table, bringing forth another burst of fury. It was mindless and useless anger, something that struck at odd times in the three days since my awakening. Just as quickly, I pulled back the reins on the emotion, and pulled them hard. I couldn't allow my emotions to run me over. I wouldn't allow myself to be the monster they said I was. My tears stopped mid-stream, my eyes drying immediately.

So hard to focus. So very damned hard to focus.

Picking up the pen again, I doodled some more, thinking some stream-of-consciousness writing would do the trick. The idea likely came from the television in the dayroom that was tuned to nothing but daytime talk shows featuring psychics, quacks, and women testing the fifteenth guy for the paternity of their child. I figured it would either work or it wouldn't. I was starting to get desperate. I needed the truth about myself. I needed to know if I actually fought monsters.

Or if I was the monster.

The door behind me opened with a metallic rustle of keys and a squalling of hinges. The heavy steps told me who it was before he even spoke. I groaned inwardly at the implications of his arrival.

"Time's up, Tom!" Jaime Dole bellowed, so happy and jovial that I wouldn't have been surprised if he was popping stuff meant for the residents. He was tall and broad, like a mental hospital orderly was supposed to be. I mean it; the dude was a shade under seven feet tall and half that wide. Somewhere, a wrestling federation was missing its champion. Short-cut blonde hair topped his head and crystal-clear blue eyes set in a fair-complected face made him seem less-threatening than I knew he was. Jaime did his best not to get physical, but he could, and he would, as he demonstrated on another patient a few hours before.

"Come on, Jaime," I whined, knowing it would do no good. "I just got started!"

"Sorry, Tom. Doctor's orders." He reached down to pick up the papers strewn across the table, giving a look of disapproval over the mess I made. Jaime made no comment on most of the intact ones, but the last page made him smile. "Drawing guitars now, huh? Funny-looking one."

I shrugged, the rage threatening to bubble up again. A few more quick breaths brought it under control. "It's a banjo," I explained, my voice a lot more calm than I felt.

Some of my disapproval must have slipped through on my voice. "Oh, sorry." Jaime straightened the papers and put them under his arm. He then held out his hand expectantly. "Give it, Tom."

"What?" I was about as convincing as a three-year-old with chocolate across his face.

"The pen. You know you can't keep it."

Dammit. I pushed the pen into his hand grudgingly. "What the hell am I going to do with a pen, man?"

"Draw a door on the wall and walk through it?" That struck us both as funny and we laughed, mine a bit more forced than his. Jaime was a good guy; I felt that. There was something else, though, and if I could get these drugs out of my system, I knew I could figure out what.

"What time is it?" I asked, rubbing my eyes. I felt like I could sleep a week.

"Your favorite time: group."

I groaned out loud. Of all the annoying things in this world I woke up in, be it the thin blankets, the threadbare carpets, the constant wind outside, bringing the snow to tap against the windows at all hours, I hated group the most. It was the absolute worst thing about being in the institution, even worse than being in it.

"Come on, Tom, you know the rules. I don't want to have to get your meds and you don't want to take them, do you?" I shook my head in defeat. "Great! Now let's go."

I shuffled out of my room, feeling I had missed something, or the opportunity for something. That feeling was ever-present in my mind for the prior three days. I shunted it to the part of my head that was clambering for news from the world. It hungered for just raw data, and I gave it what it wanted. That part of me could deal with the weird thoughts and feelings I was having. In the meantime, I would have to handle dealing with crazy people pouring out their justifications for whatever they did to get stuck in this place.

Man, I hate group therapy.

Chapter Two

My feet dragged across the cheap tile floor as I shuffled to the dayroom, where most everything horrid in this place happened. The floor was cold through the slippers I wore, just another in the long list of insults I had endured over the last three days. Each step took a bit more out of me, dragging down my spirit to the point I just wanted everything over and done.

Not for the first time, I considered the quick way out. It would have been pretty easy, too. A hangman's noose from my sheet tied off at my window, then around my neck. I dance for a few minutes before my brain stops getting oxygen, then it's off to Never Never Land. There was metal I could take from my bed and fashion a sharp object. A few minutes later, I could have my veins open to the world. From the marks already on my wrists, it didn't seem to be an original thought. Something in my head kept me from taking that route. Stubbornness was a possibility, though it was more that I didn't have the desire to really do anything. Whether it was the drugs in me or something else, I just decided to let things happen to me because I could not really care less what was going on.

Besides, I was in an asylum; someone could always just do the job for me.

The halls stretched in front of me, the lights harsh and brutal in illuminating everything. The cracks in the floor were brought out in perfect detail, bringing me more and more awake, convincing me I was not dreaming any of this. I looked at my hands and arms, goosebumps making the hair stand up straight. The cold wasn't completely to blame; it was the place Jaime was taking me. I utterly despised therapy here, group or otherwise.

Now, before anyone gets the idea I'm against people getting help when they need it, let me assure you: I'm all for it. I've seen some folks who needed help get help, and it worked for them because they wanted the help, even if it was a delayed realization. Therapy, drugs, whatever works. When you need help, get help, whatever it takes. Okay, I'm off my soapbox.

The problem was, the folks I was about to join had no desire for help. In fact, they reveled in their dysfunction.

I kept my head down, staring at the floor while my senses tried to come back to something resembling human functioning. Artificial sleep clung to my synapses, slowing me down, inside and out. Whatever they shot me up with had a hell of a lot of side-effects; I couldn't believe what I had in me was legal. I would careen back and forth between non-sensitivity to hypersensitivity. At that moment, I was going hyper, which did not bode well for me. I lost my balance for a moment, and my hand groped for the back of my seat, fingers seeming to burn on the cold metal. As I pulled myself into the chair and joined the little half-circle, causing the metal feet to shriek on the tile, I chanced a quick look at the other occupants of the dayroom.

Ava Nammon sat in her chair, her pockets bulging with odds and ends she had found, or more likely stolen, from everyone and anyone she could dupe to look the other way for however long it took to get her paws on the object of her desire. She was lanky underneath her blue sweatshirt and sweatpants, which was pretty much the uniform of the day, but I doubted whoever ran the institution planned on someone like Ava. She wore her blonde hair pulled tightly back against her skull, the tie holding her ponytail likely stolen from someone else. I could almost hear her scalp screaming from the tightness of her hair. Her ice-chip eyes flitted over everything in sight, and I could see the calculation in them. She wanted everything. Absolutely everything. That explained by why she was there: severe kleptomania. According to what I had gathered in between bouts of throwing up and waking in a cold sweat because of detoxing from the drugs they gave me, Ava Nammon had stolen with a magpie's eye. A button here, a bracelet there, a piece of machinery elsewhere. The button had had a diamond, the bracelet was a medical bracelet, and the piece of machinery was from a ventilator, all of which were her mother's. The old lady didn't last more than five minutes without the machine to breathe for her. She died because the girl couldn't keep her hands to herself, and from what Ava told me, Ava didn't give a shit. She got what she wanted.

Next to her was Tony "Bubba" Gullia, a fat, piggy-eyed bastard who needed two chairs for his massive body. When I say massive, I mean absolutely huge beyond any feasible stretch of humanity, to the point I could almost hear the seats squealing like a rust-corroded shutter in pain from his bulk. Bubba topped at least the four-hundred-pound mark if he was an ounce, the oversized sweatshirt riding up showing a pale gut whose stretch marks had stretch marks. He was bald, which did nothing but add to the impression of a mountain of flesh given life. Every time I saw him move, it was with a grace that belied his bulk, even though I still gave him as wide a berth as possible in the halls. His breathing was normal, which was decidedly weird; I half-expected him to wheeze and pant just sitting down. Bubba wore what had to be specially made shoes, as no shoes I had heard of stretched like his did. It was grotesque, to say the very least.

Indra Vivian de Dia looked for all the world like she was trying to be the most fashionable one in the room. The hell of it was, she would have accomplished it had it not been for the disgusted looks she gave everyone who came into her sight. I could hear her muttering under her breath a comment about each person. Better arms. Nicer eyes. Cleaner hair. Bigger tits. Looking into her green eyes, I could almost tell she wanted to grab bits and pieces of everyone and utterly destroy them. Considering that was what she did on the outside to get stuck in the asylum in the first place, I was glad she was in her own room, and the doors locked every night. I had no desire to wake up without my nose.

To Indra's left was Lucy. She didn't have a last name that anyone would say, and she was not going to tell. Flowing red hair that glowed with a luster, she peered down her nose at everyone. I knew her type; everyone knew someone like Lucy. She was better than you were, at anything and everything, and she would let the world know about it. It could have been performing rocket surgery on an epileptic baboon, and she would say she did it better and faster than everyone and anyone else. Flawless skin, which I guessed she somehow got some kind of product in for how it shone, and a haughty look were a bit intimidating. I hadn't said ten words to her before she dismissed me as someone not worthy of her attention. That was fine with me; I didn't have any use or time for someone that in love with themselves.

Last in the room was Doctor James Odentson, who supposedly ran the place. He wore his black hair cut short, and his smile shone with the tale of good hygiene and great dentistry. There was always an easy smile across his face, and in the two sessions of group I had attended, nothing anyone said tripped him up. He was as cool as the weather outside, and the lunatics he ran shepherd over never seemed to bother him. Under his white coat and Brooks

Brother's shirt and pants, he was built like a prize fighter. There was muscle there, and he used it on me once when I woke up from a drug-fueled nightmare. I screamed myself hoarse at things that weren't there, and when he appeared above me, I took a swing at him. He caught my fist and pushed me down on the bed so hard the wind went out of me. As I gasped for breath, his glittering blue eyes twinkled as he injected another sedative into me, and that smile never wavering. There was no doubt that he could easily do it again, at least while I was so weak; that had to change with a major quickness.

"Well, then," the doctor said, his voice smiling along with his mouth, "I guess we'll have to begin without the others. Ira is in solitary confinement after his last outburst, Ace is likely asleep, George is in individual therapy, and I've no clue where Ellen got off to." The last was met by snickers from everyone but Lucy, who did not seem to want to deign to notice anyone. "Meaning I'm not sure where she is," the doctor sighed wearily. "I do so wish you all would be somewhat couth, like Lucy and Tom over there."

That earned me a glare from the redhead. She was not one who enjoyed sharing the spotlight. I looked back blandly. I had better things to do than try and one-up some chick who thought she was shit-hot in everything. Also, my system was still processing the drugs. I couldn't have laughed if you showed me a Mel Brooks marathon.

"So let's begin, shall we?" Odentson scooted his chair to his place in the center of the half-circle, able to look at us as we could look at him. "I'm sure Ellen will slip in sometime during the session."

"That's not the only thing that slips in with her," Ava muttered, trying and failing to keep her voice low. That brought outright laughter from everyone; even Lucy let out a snort. I didn't react much as I had only seen the one called Ellen once, and I gave two-tenths of a percent of a shit about her at the time. Might have had something to do with me going through detox at the time.

"That's enough, Ava. You're already in a bit of trouble for that band in your hair." Doctor Odentson said it with about as much malice as a three-year-old could muster for a doll that fell off a shelf. It had the sound of something said so often it was by rote. He crossed his legs and put his clipboard on his knee. "Now, some of you may remember me mentioning that we would be having someone new joining us." He indicated me with a hand. "Here he is."

Indra spoke up. "He's been here before."

"Yeah, Doc," Tony said, his voice whining at a high pitch. "He's sat in group before."

Doctor Odentson nodded. "Yes, but he's much more awake now, and aware of what's going on, aren't you, Thomas?"

I perked up at the sound of my name. Honestly, I was falling asleep, and couldn't care less about the entire proceeding. Hearing my name was enough to bring me back from my thoughts, which centered around the noise of birdsong, of all things. "Yeah, totally," I said, not having any idea what I was agreeing with, and caring even less. "Absolutely."

"Christ, we gotta go through this again? He can't handle it like I can," Lucy sneered. "It was only a few ccs of morphine, you pussy."

"That will be enough of that!" Doctor Odentson's voice was a whip through the room. "Lucy, apologize."

I glanced at Lucy's face and I swear I almost saw steam vent from her ears. "For what? Calling a pussy a pussy?"

"Lucy!"

I raised my hand and saw it shaking like I was in an earthquake. "It's my fault. I'm sorry." I had no idea what I was apologizing for, but if they kept yelling, my head would explode, I would throw up, or all of the above. I was opting for the better part of valor, especially because of the piercing pain in my left temple.

"Typical pussy," Lucy smiled, a look which fit her not at all.

The doctor shook his head and continued as if nothing had happened. "Well, Thomas has come back to us, and I'm sure he'd like to get to know each of you again. Let's go around and introduce ourselves."

It was so hard keeping my head up; the phenobarbital or whatever they had pumped into my veins was still hitting the grey stuff between my ears like a hammer made of pudding. I managed to get the names again, even though the voice in the back of my head already knew the names. That little guy had been paying attention, telling me all about these folks, and how I was in likely the worst trouble I could get in my short life.

Something was wrong with the whole place, I thought as everyone did their introductions with the good grace of a pack of rabid velociraptors; group therapy had begun in earnest. I could not put my finger on it, but there was something off about the patients, the doctor, even the building itself. The voice in the back of my head went silent as I turned my head one way to the other, trying to make sense of it all.

"Now, Thomas," the doctor said, smiling, "why don't you share with us why you're here."

I shook my head. Yeah, that was going to be a negative on that.

"Come now. You'll feel much better if you let it out."

Again, I shook my head, much more violently. All aboard the NOPE-train.

"Why not? Can you at least tell us that?"

The hell of it was, I couldn't. I couldn't tell them anything. My mouth moved on its own. "You wouldn't believe me if I told you."

Lucy rolled her eyes. "Not fucking likely. I've got better reasons that you for being in here."

The pain in my head that had started on my left side drilled all the way through to the right. My hand went to my left temple, massaging it. I felt the bristles of hair that had not grown back after being shaved off. Dimly, under the rising tide of pain, I realized that was where they had placed the electrodes when they gave me the electro-shocks. There was still a slight stickiness of the gel, tacky between the hairs. My eyes screwed shut as another shiv of pain whited out my vision.

"Lucy, this isn't the time to belittle his sickness," Odentson said, caution in his voice.

"You ever think he isn't sick, you fucking quack?" Ava jumped in. "He's probably just faking it."

"I didn't need your help, Sticky Fingers," Lucy spat. "You're right, though. Maybe he's just in here because his mommy didn't want him for being such a little bitch."

My hands found my seat. Fingers wrapped around the metal legs as I leaned forward. I wasn't listening to her words. Her mouth kept opening and closing as her tongue and teeth did the dance of communication. I didn't hear her continue to insult me, calling me names, claiming I was a eunuch, telling me I deserved nothing but pain and suffering like the pain she had, that I was nothing compared to her. I heard none of that.

I was gauging the distances between my chair and her head.

"That does it!" Doctor Odentson's voice sliced through the haze of anger in front of my mind. "You are out of line, young lady, and you're going back to your room."

The cutting words stopped in an instant. "The fuck you just say?" Lucy seemed shocked at the doctor putting his foot down.

"I said, you are confined to your room. Jaime, go ahead and take her back, if you would, please."

The sudden de-escalation was a shock, bringing me out of the cold calculation that had grabbed my brain. My breathing started again, as I realized I had been holding it in preparation for the maneuver I saw in my mind.

I saw the chair flying from my hands, cracking her skull open. It would have flown true, and likely have killed her on the spot. The mental image of me leaping after it, jumping on her, slamming my fists into her haughty face over and over, was so vivid my knuckles started aching. While the anger faded like morning mist, the sight of the smile on my face, dripping with both satisfaction and her blood stayed like it was burned in with a laser. Some part of me wanted her, wanted her bones broken, her flesh ripped apart. Some part of me wanted to utterly destroy her, and would feel good doing it.

What the hell kind of monster am I?

Chapter Three

Thankfully, group ended just after that incident. The doctor thought Lucy had made some real progress, even with her "outburst", as he called it. I didn't make mention of anything, and I did nothing other than try to put my vision of Lucy violently dismembered out my head, the pieces of her displayed in alphabetical order. Even though I only had three days of memories, I could not believe I was that kind of man.

That kind of animal.

According to the clock, it was almost noon. We were pushed to our rooms for the meal, which mattered little to me. My stomach was churning from group, and I wanted nothing more than to stay in my room and put everything that I could together. The door clicked closed behind me and I sat down, thinking hard about what happened in the dayroom.

The anger was gone. The rage had vanished like it never existed. What was more, that spike of hot pain through my skull, like Elvis, had left the building. I hadn't felt anyone give me an injection of something, and no pills either, so the pain leaving without a trace was unexpected and very much odd. All that was left was that freeze-frame of me straddling the defenseless form of Lucy, my fists the color of her hair. I swallowed down the bile that wanted to come up from the thought. I couldn't be like that, could I?

The tray slot at the bottom of my door opened, and my tray was pushed into my room . I ignored the scraping of the plastic against the floor as I tried focusing on the Great Before, as in before I woke up with conductive gel on my temples and a seemingly permanent resident of the Screwloose Hotel. There had to be something there, even a hint of who I was. All I could see was white. Not white like the color, but white like a blinding flashlight in your eyes, only so much brighter.

You aren't ready for it, came that little voice in the back of my head. You probably won't ever be, at the rate you're going.

"What am I not ready for?" I asked aloud, willing that voice to answer again. It felt like the only ally I had in the entire world.

Don't talk out loud! It shouted, making me wince. They'll hear you. Besides, only crazy people talk to themselves.

I only had to be told once. So what do I do? I asked.

First, get that tray. The machine needs fuel, and you are a machine.

Obediently, I opened my eyes and went to get the tray. On it was a piece of chicken, some small whole potatoes, and greens of some sort. The good news was it looked edible. The bad news was "edible" could be a very subjective term.

Don't worry how it looks or tastes, the voice said, gruff and without any mercy. Eat it, get your strength back. You still have a ton of that shit still in your system. The food will help get it out of you faster. You don't have the time to screw around with the natural way.

How do you know so much? I asked.

How do you know so little? Snapped the voice. Haven't you been paying attention?

I don't know what's going on! Even in my head, I heard the whining tone, wheedling and weak.

You better learn fast then, boy. Now, eat that slop and get some rest. Time is not our friend here.

Who the hell are you?

The voice was silent.

I picked up the chicken and took a bite. It was a bit overcooked and dry, so I filled up one of the plastic cups with water. I chewed and swallowed, trying to force myself to keep eating. The water was cold, washing down the food and hydrating me. I didn't realize just how thirsty I was until I had guzzled two more cups. The potatoes were mushy, the greens the consistency of wet paper. Still, I dutifully chewed and swallowed, chasing the horrid meal with water as much as possible, mostly just to get the taste from my mouth.

My stomach tried to rebel and throw it all up, so terrible was the flavor, but that voice in my head was adamant. Keep it down, it said, each word a hammer strike. The way it sounded, it had the tone of someone who hated. Hated me, hated where it was, hated where I was… Just hated everything. Keeping the meal down was my attempt to make the voice happier. All I seemed to want was a simple kind word, some acknowledgement I wasn't some kind of gibbering monster, waiting for the chance to unleash horror upon whoever happened to be in attendance.

Apparently, I should have wished for the moon as the voice directed me to start counting to five hundred. When I asked why, it snarled back at me to mind my own business and it would tell me when it was damned good and ready. I sat on my bed and counted, obedient and servile. It felt better to be that way; not necessarily right, but definitely better.

About halfway to five hundred, I realized two things. One, that the light had changed dramatically, and darkness had fallen. Two, I had stopped counting because I was laying on the hard stone ground. I squeezed my eyes shut and opened them, trying to discover what happened. When I looked, my throat locked the scream on the inside of my lungs.

Blood and bodies everywhere. I was curled up in the center of a clearing in the carnage, the corpses around me in a loose circle, their life dripping away from them drop by drop. Everything was dark past the dead, but was lit perfectly for me to see every detail, every tiny bit of terror wrought on these people surrounding me.

I sat up slowly, the air seeming to have the consistency of mud. My knees were pulled up to my chest and I wrapped my arms around them, trying to close my eyes, wanting to close them, begging my locked brain to allow them to close so I could no longer see the accusatory faces, blaming me for what was done to them, for the gaping holes in their chests, the blood painting them in shades of scarlet and crimson. My eyes stayed open, stubbornly, in defiance of my wishes, devouring every detail, from the coarse black hair to the hollow eyes of a corpse too long unburied to the ashen skin streaked with not only red ichor, but white flecks of bone and torn pink tissue that might once have been a lung. The edges of the lung were jagged, like the edges of ground beef that has been pulled apart.

It took me a moment to see that the mangled chests were moving.

With a parody of life, the bodies began to stand. With my voice locked behind my teeth, I watched these men dressed in simple loincloths and feather talismans get to their feet, still surrounding me. Still these things that were once men circled me, looking down on me in silent, still vigil. One of them looked me in the eye, no expression and nothing human in its gaze. It pointed at me with its left hand, the flesh looking like rats had taken a bit of a snack from it. It then lifted its right hand high above its head, the gaze never wavering, never lessening its baleful glare on me.

In its upraised hand was a wickedly sharp obsidian knife.

I sat bolt upright in my bed, my breathing fast, harsh and painful. Around me was the same room as before, though it actually was dark this time, and I could feel the cold night coming. Laying back and taking deep breaths, I tried getting myself back under control, back into somewhat of a better state of mind, or at least as good as it would get in an asylum.

After several moments, I felt a bit better. Looking at the spot where the tray had been pushed in earlier, I saw another tray, this time with some kind of beef as the main course. The potatoes and greens were there as well, and looking just as appetizing, which made my stomach churn. A small burp of bile in the back of my throat burned, and I still nearly let my stomach empty. My mouth was dry, as if cotton was used to clean out my mouth. My head was fuzzy, as was my sight. I took off my shoes and socks so I could get under the covers and go to sleep properly. It had not been a good day, and I knew I needed rest. Whatever the voice wanted me to do could wait until morning.

The door slammed open, the metal rebounding on the outside of my room. Harsh bright light spilled in, searing my eyes and bringing a cry from my throat. I held up my hands in a warding gesture, trying to blot out the glare. Shadows flowed into the room, surrounding me. A rough hand grabbed my arm, joined by another pair of hands, squeezing around my wrists and forearms. I flailed my legs, trying to get these things away from me, trying to keep them off me. An arm snaked around my throat and a foul-tasting rag went into my mouth.

My sweatshirt was torn from my body as I was dragged outside into the hall. I tried screaming for help, but it was no use; the gag worked too well, muffling the cries locked in my throat. Still I struggled, trying to break free. Gooseflesh covered my exposed arms and chest as I was carried and dragged through what seemed like miles of hallways and back staircases to what could only be a basement.

There wasn't much to see as it was dark; the lights either weren't there or weren't yet turned on. I could hear the ticking of a water heater or a furnace nearby, though in the twilight distance was relative. Beneath my bare feet, I could feel the dirty cold stone that made up the floor of the basement. It was like no one had swept it in decades, the filth was so thick. It wasn't as cold down there, thanks to the heater, but that was a small comfort; I couldn't see where I was or what was going on.

I was thrown roughly to the floor, the sweat caused by my struggles allowing dirt and muck and dust to stick to me when I rolled to a stop. Laying there, my body chilled from the stone, I took several deep breaths, trying to get my bearings. I tried to think why I had been abducted, and why I was down in a dark, dank sublevel of a building for the insane.

The only explanation I could come up with was I was dreaming. I couldn't believe that the place was so shoddy that anyone could break into another's room and kidnap them to do whatever they wanted to them. That sounded like just something out of a bad movie. It was a dream, then. It had to be a dream.

That theory went out the window as I felt a foot connect with my ribcage. The bones creaked dangerously close to breaking and the breath exploded out of me. As I tried gulping some kind of air back into my lungs, another kick landed in my stomach, causing me to wretch uncontrollably. Bile worked its way back up my throat, accompanied by the dregs of whatever was still in my stomach. The noxious mix spattered from my mouth to the cold stone floor, the acidic taste burning my insides. My arms couldn't hold me and I fell face-first into my own vomit, inhaling some of it as I tried to gain my bearings; the stomach acid burned my nostrils.

I rolled onto my back, then continued rolling twice more, trying to buy myself time. Time to think, time to plan, time to prepare; I couldn't say. All I accomplished was getting just enough air back into my lungs to let out a mewling cry. A harsh uncovered bulb, one of four lights I could see, swung above my head. It was almost hypnotic, swaying back and forth, that I nearly forgot what had put me on the ground in the first place. My breathing slowed from the hitching gulps of air to an almost-regular rhythm, and I almost felt at peace.

Move! The voice in my head screamed, snapping me out of my reverie. I tried to move, tried to roll, tried to pull myself into a ball. My success was limited, as the kick only fetched to the left side of my head. I covered my head with my hands, feebly trying to protect myself from the flurry of blows that hammered into me like a tidal wave of pain. A heel connected solidly with my temple, bringing a tortured cry of pain from my throat. The world grayed out for a moment, reality losing its consistency more than it already had.

I felt my mental self roughly pushed to the side as the voice rocketed to the forefront, a roar of anger and rage bellowing from me. I saw my hands leave off from protecting my head to grabbing at the heavy shoe kicking at me. The fingers grazed the laces and the foot caught me in the eye, bringing a bright flare of new pain to my already tortured body.

The rage burning through my blood did not die down from the vicious attack; on the contrary, it actually fueled the voice to grab again. This time my hands succeeded, wrapping like a vice on the offending limb. With what seemed like practiced ease, my attacker's foot stomped to the floor, my left arm underneath it. I cried out in a mixture of pain and rage as my attacker ground my wrist, twisting his foot. I was on my left side, tears running down my face, as I beat at the leg ineffectually. I might as well have been trying to cut down the largest tree in the forest with my bare hands for all the good it did.

My assailant stood over me, then dropped. I barely had time to brace myself as his full weight landed on my stomach, making me retch again. Though my hands were free, all of my limbs were useless as fists sailed down at my face and head, striking like steel hammers, rocking my head into the stone floor with each blow. I brought my arms up to try covering my head, which did little to stop the attack. The punches became just flailing blows, the thumps against me not damaging anymore. It was as the blows became less damaging that I heard the noise coming from my attacker.

Laughter. He was laughing at me, and had been the entire time. From the moment I had been kicked in the ribs, he had been laughing. It wasn't a happy laugh, either; it was the laugh of disgust and derision, as if he couldn't stand even the look of me and enjoyed trying to destroy what he considered inferior. Whether it lasted a minute, an hour, or a year, I couldn't tell. All I wanted was for the pain to stop.

A raspy voice rang through the room. "That's enough, Ira!"

The voice caused me to let down my guard, my hands coming down from my face. That allowed one final blow to strike me in the forehead, bouncing the back of my head off the stone and again into the fist. Stars flew across my sight, and I covered my head again. I felt the not-inconsiderable weight of Ira lift off my stomach, giving me a farewell kick to the ribs. My breath came in gasps as I rolled onto my left side again, curling into a fetal position. I hitched in air, which brought on a whole other symphony of agony. I tried not to cry, but trying just wasn't good enough.

"Fucking pussy," Ira said. His voice was a cheese grater, making my ears wince. "Couldn't take a few punches. What a little bitch." I opened the only eye I could to take a look at him, since the right one was nearly fused shut. Ira wasn't that tall, at least I didn't think he was; my view of him from the ground didn't allow for much perspective. His shirt was off, showing off rippling muscles on a whipcord-thin body. There was a sheen of sweat that glistened in the swinging cone of light from the nearest bulb hanging from the ceiling. Ira was completely bald, the only hair on him seeming to be his blonde eyebrows. "I should work on him a bit more, toughen him up a bit." The smile on his face was completely devoid of anything human. His pale eyes were haunting, looking at me as if I was little more than scum under his shoe, or some other lower form of life. My eye slipped shut.

The first voice was stern, steel wrapped in velvet. "You've done more than enough, Ira." I felt hands on me again, this time gentle and non-threatening. I wept openly, the first sense of kindness I had been shown in what felt like centuries. The hands were strong as they guided me to my feet, and the arms encircled me, keeping me upright. My right arm went around his neck, my hand clutching at my savior's shirt like a sailor lost at sea. "You know the rules."

"Fuck the rules," Ira spat, the venom almost a solid blow against my ears. "Bitch can't hang, he can't hang."

"You want the doctor to come down on us?"

There was a snort, but this time I heard a note of fear, or at least unease. I heard three stomps and felt a pair of rough hands on the side of my face. "You better not say one damned word to anybody, bitch. This is just for us. You understand?" When I didn't say anything, my head was nodded for me, the bones in my neck creaking and cracking under the abuse, my brain sloshing back and forth in my skull. "I will fuck you up beyond all recognition if you say a damned word, bitch. Your boyfriend won't stop me from making you fucking suffer."

The steel voice was near my ear, and it brooked no argument. "I said that's enough, Ira, or would you rather I answer you in kind?" When the hands left my face, I could hear the nod in the voice. "That's what I thought. We're going now."

"Whatever," came the disinterested reply. "You'll be back."

I felt myself being half-carried, half-guided forward, not seeing anything in front of me. My head hung forward lankly, all my strength going to keeping me from falling flat on my already-abused face. Each breath I took brought a grinding sensation in my ribs, so I took tiny sips of air. My feet scuffed against the floor, and with each step, my guardian urged me on gently but incessantly. The whispers of encouragement were a salve for my soul, and I felt my spirits start to lift.

Before I could say anything, we came to an abrupt stop, bringing a hiss of pain from me and a muttered curse from the man keeping me vertical. I gritted my teeth, trying to stop my legs from unhinging and spilling me to the floor. That I didn't just collapse was a testament to the guy holding me up. "Hold on, Tom. I'll do the talking." I kept my head down and said nothing. Even though I had just been beaten to a pulp, I had enough sense to keep my mouth shut.

"Hey, George," came a jocular voice. There was too much happiness in the words, almost forced to the point of insincerity. "Who've you got there?"

"It's Tom, as you can plainly see, Milton." The one called George sounded bored, but the voice in my head could tell there was an underlying current of concern. "He fell down some stairs."

"Is that right?" Another voice, just as insincere but with a deeper pitch, came from my left. "Ain't that a shame?"

"It sure is, Dante," Milton said, syrupy sweetness coming from every word. "I don't know, George. Those don't look like bruises from falling."

"Yeah, and how did he find the stairs? Answer me that, Georgey."

George took a deep breath to say something. I beat him to it.

"I was sleepwalking." The words were slurred, whether from pain or the sudden wave of fatigue that flowed over me. I had no idea I was going to say anything, let alone a bald-faced lie. "I don't know what happened. I woke up on the floor at the bottom of the stairs."

The voice in the back of my head seemed to like my story, even going so far as to give me a mental nod of approval.

"Sleepwalking?" Dante sounded skeptical. "Doc didn't say anything about you sleepwalking."

George took over. "With all the drugs in his system along with the shocks he's gotten, he's lucky he doesn't think he's Jesus Christ." He squeezed my shoulder, likely trying to keep me quiet. "Cut him some slack. I'll get him back to his room."

"I dunno." Milton's words dripped into my ear like poisoned honey. "I think the doc should know all about this."

I felt George shake his head slowly. "Okay, boys. What's it gonna cost this time?" There was a long pause, then Dante spat out the name Ellen. I felt George's arms thrum with anger as he said "She's her own person. You can ask her, though what she'd want with either of you escapes me."

"Come on, George," Milton said. "You know she wants it."

"I make no promises, and you two are asking for quite a bit more than you ever should. Why the doctor allows you to stay on is beyond me."

"Good thing it's not up to you, Georgey." Milton licked his lips, at least that was what it sounded like, and said, "So how about it?"

"It's her choice. I can't make her choices for her. She has free will." George paused.

That isn't true, said the voice in my head, and you know it isn't true.

"Well?" I could hear the anticipation in Dante's single word.

"I'll ask her. That's all I will do. Deal?"

"Fine, George, and we didn't see anything. Right, Dante?"

"Right you are, Milton!" I could almost see the tip of the invisible cap Dante gave. It was just such the smart-ass response the guy would give. "Just make sure you're back in your room by breakfast, George."

We began moving again, and I started drifting. My head-roommate fell into silence, whether from lack of anything to say or the same exhaustion in which I found myself drowning. After what seemed like hours, I felt myself put into what felt like the softest, warmest bed ever. Sure, it was the same bed I was forcibly torn from only perhaps an hour before, but it felt like absolute heaven. My head touched the pillow gently and I felt the blanket drawn over me.

"Sleep, Tom," came George's voice from the end of the longest tunnel at the end of the deepest well. "You'll need the rest."

I felt my mouth form the word "Why?"

"Help comes in different forms, Tommy. I'll help you as long as you help yourself. Now shut up and get some sleep."

I wanted to argue. I wanted to know what he meant. I wanted a lot of things, but my body apparently wanted to listen to George more than it did my own wishes. Within seconds I was out.

And I dreamed.

Chapter Four

Dreams are funny things. Not just funny ha-ha, but funny as in you have no idea what to expect. No one knows why people dream. Some think it's a way for the brain to get rid of any problem thoughts and ideas. Others say it might be a doorway to a realm of either shared consciousness with the rest of the world, or a solo mental playground that lasts just as long as sleeping does.

I had no real opinion on the matter. My nights had been dreamless since I woke up in the chair, empty of any thought besides a blackness that swallowed me from the moment my head hit the pillow to the second Jaime woke me up the next morning. I never woke up during the night, as least not that I could tell, and I never remembered anything when I woke up. In the morning, I would always wake up rested, but empty, as if I were missing something. I knew what dreaming was; I just had not had any I could remember.

Bright light beat down on my closed eyelids, along with a warmth that suffused my entire body. I felt softness beneath me as I lay on my back, my hands touching what felt like cloth. There was singing in the distance, something I knew I should remember, but it was faint, too far away to really make sense of the words. Whatever the song was, it was pleasant to my ears, filling me with contentment. That was my first clue I was dreaming; feeling content didn't really seem to be my lot in life.

My second clue was the complete lack of pain. The creaking of my ribs whenever I took a breath was gone, as was the drilling spikes from being kicked in the temple. My wrist was innocent of any kind of discomfort, and my stomach wasn't roiling after emptying what little I had eaten. Some could argue that the beating I took was the dream and the peaceful awakening was reality. A fair statement, but considering the amount of abuse I took, a dream could not hurt that badly without waking up the dreamer. I knew the difference. I wasn't sure how I knew, but I knew it quite clearly.

Taking a chance, I opened my eyes, and immediately regretted it. The light was intense, a sledgehammer on my senses. My eyes closed on their own, squeezing so tightly water flowed from them. After a moment, I squinted, letting light come in a little at a time, like I was stepping into a cold swimming pool on a blistering hot day. Slowly I realized I could see blue above me, the richest and deepest blue I could remember. Admittedly, my memory didn't go very far, but it was still the most absolutely gorgeous thing I had ever seen. The light was the sun, something I didn't expect to see ever again from my cell at the institution. I luxuriated in the warmth, letting it fill my pores, praising the rays falling on me, renewing my soul.

After a few moments, I sat up and confirmed I was dreaming.

I propped myself up on my elbows, looking down on the shore of a lake. I recognized it, or almost did. Something important had happened on that shore, and I knew I wanted to remember. From where I lay, I could see the crystal water, the emerald grass waving in the soft breeze, the trees clawing for the blameless blue sky, covering the shoreline three-quarters the way around the lake. Leaves of all different shades of green covered the branches of the trees, swaying in the wind, gently whispering to me, to the world, to themselves.

There was a blanket underneath me; checkered in blue and white, it had the feel of freshly washed and often used. I bunched up the cloth in my hands, and it was smooth, like cotton. I couldn't tell what it was made of, really, nor did I think it really mattered. The pattern was soothing with its orderly progression of blue and white squares, as if all was right in the universe, and one thing followed another, just as it was supposed to do. I rolled onto my right side and let my fingers trace the pattern, one square at a time.

I chuckled at myself. Some dream of flying, some dream of world domination. I dream of summer vacation. As I lay back on the blanket, I felt my eyes start to slip closed. I was so relaxed because I knew I was dreaming. Nothing could hurt me there. I could and would feel no pain. There was nothing to fear, nothing to hurt me, nothing that would hurt me. That was how I knew it was a dream; there was no other place in the universe I could ever feel that safe and secure.

"That's not true, you know."

The voice whipped out from nearby, off to my left. I rolled onto my stomach and stood up, my movement about as coordinated as a pregnant yak. Standing there, wearing a long black coat in spite of the beautiful weather, black jeans, and old-fashioned sneakers, was a man looking at me with utter disdain. His brown hair was a bit long, his eyes were a dark brown, and he looked about my height. There was what seemed to be a permanent scowl on his face, wrinkling his forehead and turning down the corners of his mouth.

He could have used a shave, the stubble not that flattering. The coat covered his body, so I couldn't tell whether he was fat or thin, muscular or scrawny, and he kept the coat closed, his hands shoved into the pockets. I stepped back from the baleful glare coming from this man, who looked for all the world as if he wanted to rip me limb from limb.

"No, I won't do that," he said, heaving a huge sigh, the kind people use with small children or adults with the attitude of a small child. "You need to pull your head out of your ass."

"Who are you?" It was the only thing I could think to say.

There was an eyeroll, then, "Use that thing in your skull for something besides keeping your ears apart. Who the hell do you think I am?"

I shrugged my shoulders, starting to lose interest in this visitor. If he wasn't going to hurt me, then I couldn't find a reason to care about him. Out of sight, out of mind. I turned back toward the lake, letting the tranquility soothe me after the arrival of this oafish and probably cruel creature. When I looked back, he was gone. Even the grass where he stood looked perfectly undisturbed. I returned my attention to the water.

The waves lapping at the shore of the lake brought me peace as I settled back onto the blanket. I couldn't care any less about the stranger if I tried. The lake stayed crystal blue, the grass stayed emerald green, and the sky remained clear. I didn't care if I ever woke up, because I was finally at peace.

Something in that blameless sky caught my eye. A small cloud floated up there, and it looked so lonely. A small smile crossed my lips as I considered just how alike we were. Neither of us had anyone else, and that was unlikely to change. I sighed as I sat up, leaning back on my hands. At least since I was alone, I wouldn't have to worry about hurting anyone else.

"This is a dream, Tommy. You'll have to wake up sometime."

The voice was different this time. Much different, in that it was a woman's voice. The only female voices I had heard recently were at group, and this was not one of them. It was a sweeter voice, one I felt I should know but couldn't quite place. I started to turn around.

"Don't turn around, Tommy. You don't need to see me. I'm not going to hurt you." I stayed where I was, sitting and watching the waves on the lake. "I just need you to listen."

"You aren't going to tell me who you are, are you?"

There was a short, brittle laugh. "No, but then, I won't have to."

I leaned forward, legs crossed, chin cupped in my hands. "More riddles. Great."

"You don't like riddles?" The voice came closer. I heard the footsteps on grass getting closer to me before stopping a few feet behind me.

"They make my head hurt, and I don't like to hurt." I sounded petulant, like a child, and I didn't care. Trying to figure things out made me tired, and made my head pound. "I guess you'll just say something cryptic and disappear."

"No, Tommy, I won't." Whoever she was, she sat down behind me. "I'm just going to keep you company for a little while, until you figure it out."

"And if I never figure it out?"

"You will. You're smart like that."

We sat in silence for some time, whether it was a minute, an hour, a lifetime; the passage of time in dreams is never a constant.

"Why can't I see you?"

The answer was immediate. "Those are the rules."

"Why? It's my dream. I should be able to do what I want."

"So why would you dream someone telling you to do something, then do what it says?"

That stumped me for a minute, and I puzzled over it. When no easy solution presented itself, I pushed it away. It didn't matter.

"You give up too easily," she chided. Her next statement was on a completely different tangent. "Do you know why you're here?"

I hesitated before whispering, "Because I killed people."

"Are you sure?"

For days I had wrestled with that question. Had I really killed someone, let alone multiple someones? Did I have blood on my hands, or was it just some sick mental game my mind was playing on me? Eventually, I decided on an answer. "If I hadn't, I wouldn't be in the institution."

I could almost hear the shrug in her shoulders. "Yes," she said, "that does make a bit of sense, doesn't it?"

"Yeah." I felt proud that I had figured something out, and promptly let the feeling go. "Does that bother you?"

She let out a smothered chuckle. "What, that you've killed people?" I nodded at her question, keeping myself facing forward. "No. I'm sure you had good reason for doing it."

I hunched forward, my guilt heavy on my conscience. "I didn't. I shot a man in the head and I don't know why I did it."

"Are you sure?" Those words again.

"That's what my file says. Why would they lie?"

Another chuckle sounded from behind me as she repeated my words. "Why would they lie?" I heard her stand up. "Our time's almost done. Look up."

I did so, and saw the cloud was a lot closer. It was heavier and darker than when I last saw it, spreading like a bruise on the skin of the sky. That was a cloud that promised rain by the buckets and lightning enough to make Zeus himself call it a bit much.

There was a mental double-take, so strong it made my neck hurt from the whiplash. Why would that comparison come to mind? There were no gods. That's what the doctor kept telling me. The gods were nothing but something in my head to justify the killing. Zeus was not real.

"What is that?" I pointed at the cloud, as if anyone could mistake me asking about the trees or the lake. They were perfect. That storm cloud was not.

"It's pain, Tommy. It is pain I wish you didn't have to feel, and I would take it from you if I could." Sadness swept through her voice, and it was fading away as the wind picked up very suddenly. "I've got to go now."

"Can we talk again?" I shouted the words, my eyes locked onto the coming storm.

"We will. Just listen."

The rain started then, with drops the size of quarters falling from the sky. It was a cold rain, each raindrop hitting me bringing up gooseflesh. I was drenched in seconds. "To what?"

Lightning struck the lake, the electricity crackling across the water, arcing from one wave to the next. The peal of thunder was a solid mass, and with the help of the battering wind and torrential downpour forced me to fall on my back. My breath escaped me, and I involuntarily inhaled a mouthful of rain as I tried to get it back. I rolled onto my side and tried to get the water out of my mouth before I choked. My ribs ached from the effort, creaking as if someone had tried to kick them in. Lightning crashed again, the thunder drilling through my head like a spike. I howled in terror, my voice lost in the symphony of natural disaster.

I rolled onto my stomach, getting another nose full of water before I could get to my knees. Pushing myself to my feet was no easy task, but I managed to do it in spite of the rain and thunder and wind. For a moment I stood there, proud of my achievement, for the first time actually feeling good about myself.

That lasted up until I felt the hair on my arms stand up.

The smell of ozone was first, then came the buzzing, like bees, but the sound was coming from inside my head. I felt the muscles in my limbs tense tightly just before I was blown off my feet by a bolt of lightning. The pain was immediate, and I screamed as I landed after skidding through the grass. There was a thrumming in my chest, which I hoped was my heart still beating. My arms and legs were useless as I just laid there, unable to move, my eyes blinded by the streak of hot electricity that had hit right in front of me.

As the sky split apart again, the last word I heard was "Yourself".

And then lightning struck again.

Chapter Five

Everyone's seen the movies. When someone has a bad dream, they sit up, soaked in sweat, a scream locked behind their teeth, breathing heavily and thankful that, no matter what, the worst was left in their subconscious. They would lay back down, letting their racing heart get back under control. Staring at the ceiling would be the next thing, along with muttered prayers of thanks and sighs of relief. After they get themselves under control, they get up, get some water, go do their thing in the bathroom, and fall back asleep. Of course, that is exactly what I did.

Well, minus the sitting up, the laying back down, the getting up, and the water. It hurt too much to move. The scream didn't amount to much more than a plaintive whine, my body crying out in sheer agony from tensing while waking up. I think I raised up an entire quarter-inch before pure pain sent me right onto my back. That just added to the abuse, the mattress being about as thick as a beach towel, and covering steel slats. I hurt so badly even thinking about curling up into a ball was unimaginable.

"About time you woke up, Tommy," came a familiar voice. My relatively uninjured eye rolled to the sound. It was George, my brain said, hammering through the pain. My beating at the hands of Ira came back to me, the memory fresh and painful as an open wound on a salt lick. "I almost thought you weren't coming back." No light of any kind came through my window, meaning it was still night or the snow had covered it, or both. The light in my room was on, illuminating enough for me to finally get a look at him. He was younger than me, dark-skinned with a cap of wiry hair. An off-white robe covered him, drawn mostly closed with a faded yellow belt around his middle, and I could see the baby-blue pajamas underneath. George reached for me with wide fingers on enormous hands. I shrank away from him as much as I could, which amounted to not at all. His eyes were brown, but the pupils were open so wide there was almost no iris. It's funny the things people notice when they're in abject pain and terror.

Though they looked clumsy, George's hands were gentle as he rolled me over onto my stomach. I felt pressure through my shirt in the middle of my back, then a twist. There was an instant of pain, then blessed relief radiated out. I let out a sigh and realized I could turn my head. I did so, trying to look at George as he did whatever he was doing.

He cracked his knuckles, which went off like firecrackers, and began to knead his palms into my left arm at the shoulder. Again, the moment of agony was replaced by euphoria, the sensation flowing all the way down the limb and joining the oasis in at the center of my back. I experimentally moved my fingers, trying to make sure I could still feel them. That was when I realized I could see out of both my eyes.

"What---?" I tried to say, but managed no better than a croak.

"Hush, Tommy." George moved to my left leg, starting at my hip and doing some kind of jab at the back of my thigh. "This is exacting work, and I'm already behind. I couldn't do it while you were asleep." I remained silent. "Good. You do listen." He had passed from my sight and I didn't want to move at all. Another poke with his stone fingers to my calf was accompanied by high pressure to the sole of my foot. The aches on my left side vanished completely.

"Now, this is going to suck," George muttered. "Hang on." With gentle, steady pulls, he moved the bed away from the wall so he could get to my right side. I whimpered a bit from the movement, but not as much as I thought I would. Once he had room, he repeated his actions, this time faster and with more confidence. After what seemed like only a minute or two, he went back to where I assumed he was sitting before I woke up. "Better? See if you can sit up."

Slowly and gingerly, I pushed myself up. The pain was there, but much lessened, like a ghost of a memory of pain. My breathing was no longer labored, and I actually did sit up, my hands on the edge of the bed, my feet on the cold stone floor.

"Thank you," I whispered.

George shook his head. "Don't thank me yet. You have a long way to go."

Muscles in my chest twitched, sending a small wave of discomfort down to my feet. "What are you talking about?"

"Ira will want another shot at you."

"I don't even know him!" I hissed. "Why does he hate me so much?"

"It's what you did before," George shrugged. "The good news is it's not business. It's personal."

My right arm went protectively across my chest. I felt phantom feet kicking me in the ribs, and George's magic fingers did not take the memory away. "How the heck is that good news?"

"It means he wants you at the top of your game for the next time." George smiled at that. "That gives us time."

"But I don't want to fight him, or anyone, for that matter." I laid back down on my side, keeping George in view. "What about the doctor?"

"He has an idea, but nothing he can say outright." George massaged his own hands as if they had lost circulation. "Ira is good at what he does, and the orderlies couldn't give a damn less. They're new, and they seem like they enjoy the fights as much as Ira does."

My brain wasn't having any of it. "I can't believe there's some guy who gets away with beating people up here! That is insane!"

George laughed at that. "You do realize where you are, right?" That brought me up short. "Doesn't matter, though. Ira is still going to come after you, and you need to be ready."

I shook my head, the rough material of the mattress scratching my shorn head. "I don't want to do it. I'm not a fighter. I'm a killer, and I don't want to hurt anyone again."

"He will kill you." The finality in George's voice sunk through me like ice. "He will kill you or worse."

I focused on George, and the question was pulled out of me. "What's worse than death?"

"Spending the rest of your life as a vegetable. Won't ever get out of here if that happens."

"Why am I supposed to get out? I'm here for a reason."

George stood, brushing wrinkles from his robe. "Oh, I know you are, Tommy. I know you are." He made his way to my door, which was slightly open. "I have to get back to my room. The rules here are for safety." George rolling his eyes told me all I needed to know about what he thought of the rules. "I'll be back in a few hours. It's the weekend, so we have some time to work on things and for you to heal up."

I chuckled, the first time I laughed without any pain in what seemed like forever. "Ira takes days off?"

"Milton and Dante like to put him in solitary, just to keep him angry." George gripped the door handle and paused before leaving. "Get some sleep. You're going to need it."

The door closed, cutting off the dim light from the hall. I rolled onto my back, looking up at the pock-marked ceiling and marveling at the lack of pain, and my ability to look out through both eyes. Ira had worked me over pretty thoroughly, and probably would have killed me if George hadn't stepped in. That told me something, but my tired brain was completely uninterested in finding out what.

I turned on my left side, staring at the wall as my eyelids began to droop. I was in the middle of deciding I should think about asking George what was going on when I was unceremoniously thrown out of bed, hearing a loud "Rise and shine!" after I hit the floor. My blanket fell over my face as I let out a cry of surprise. Pulling the cloth away, I saw the light had changed considerably, slanting through the iron-grill covered window high above.

Great. I hate flash-forwards. Losing time is not one of my favorite things. I must have been tired, which made some sense. After all, being beaten within an inch of your life can really tucker someone out. Granted, a warm glass of milk or counting sheep is a better way to get to sleep, but it wasn't like I had a say in the matter.

Heavy footsteps came from behind me, and as I turned my head and looked, I caught the back of one of the orderlies. It wasn't Jaime who dumped me like that; he didn't have the temperament to do something that mean. The guy who left was just as big and broad, what people would say either a linebacker or a brick wall should look like. His reddish-blonde hair was faded to a bristle-cut on the top of his head, showing off the reddened neck of someone who looked like they worked in the fields for months at a time. Other details filtered in from the few seconds I saw him leave, but I couldn't process or even understand all of them.

Milton or Dante, the voice inside whispered. They get off on that kind of thing.

What kind of thing? I asked.

Being a dickhead, came the swift and silent response. Also, Jaime doesn't walk with a limp in his left leg. It's likely an injury from a long time ago. He doesn't even know he's limping unless someone tells him. Carries himself like a professional bully.

Getting up from the stone floor, I started making my bed, more to give myself something to do instead of standing there doing nothing while talking to myself. How do you know? I said inside.

Process of elimination. Dressed like an orderly. Not Jaime. Pretty self-explanatory. The other stuff is just noticing, looking, observing what is around you. It's not rocket science. It's just opening your eyes.

I tucked the sheets in. Who are you?

My ears inside heard a deep heaving sigh. You'll figure it out.

That's what she said.

There was a burst of laughter from the voice then it went serious. Wait, who said that?

My bed was made, so I got dressed for the day in the usual sweatshirt and sweatpants. They were a one size fits all, and even in the middle of my internal conversation, I felt wrong with the uniformity. The lady in my dream, after you left she said I would figure it out.

I felt rather than heard the simmering anger coming from my mental passenger. "Can't leave well enough alone," the voice muttered.

What does that mean? I asked, trying to get an idea of why he was so mad. I wasn't feeling as scared of him as before; after having the crap beaten out of me in the real world, the potential for attacks by a voice in my head didn't have the same effect.

A knock sounded at my door, and I glanced up. Jaime stood there, smiling as always. He twisted his way through the doorway, his shoulders not allowing him to just walk directly in. "Great! You're already up. Come on, Tommy. Time to get moving!"

"Where am I going now?" I asked, trying to orient on exactly where I was being taken. "It isn't time for group. We had group yesterday."

"Better! You get to talk to the doctor. Time for your one-on-one."

Good, the voice inside said. We can get this show on the road.

What show? Can't you just give me a hint? I asked as I said out loud, "Okay. I guess I don't have a choice."

"You always have a choice, Tommy. It's just easier on me and you and everyone else if you go along with it." Jaime's smile dimmed slightly. "It also means I don't have to sedate you and put you in solitary. Ira's been in there constantly for months. He really has some issues."

Jaime's words said a lot to me, and I put him in the "clueless" category. I doubted he knew what went on the night before; his words and demeanor were at odds with knowledge of a fistfighting arena in the bowels of a sanitarium. He was only the day shift, and was oblivious to what happened at night. Either that or he missed his calling as a professional poker player and actor. There was an innocence to him, at least as far as what Milton and Dante were doing, but I felt he had something else going on. What it was, I couldn't say, but it was there, just below the surface. Given enough time, I could likely figure it out. For the moment, though, I was holding up progress as Jaime crossed his arms and waited, leaning against the doorjamb. He looked prepared to stand there all day waiting for me. Of course, he likely would have picked me up, tucked me under one arm, and just carried me, but I didn't want to give him reason to do that.

I pulled on my slippers and stood. Something had awakened a curiosity inside me, a desire to know, for the first time, what was happening around me. More, I wanted to know what was being done to me. There was more going on than met the eye; of that much I was sure. I just needed to find out what.

"Okay, Jaime," I said. "Don't want to keep the good doctor waiting."

Chapter Six

The institution was just as dreary in the day as the evening, although it was much more bearable when stoned to the gills on whatever they put in their needles. If I didn't have to deal with the after-effects, I would have asked for a Nembutal or two, just to take the edge off.

Harsh white light bore down from the ceiling, making me squint my eyes against the glare. Whether that was from being in the dark for so long or a remnant of the drugs from however long they were in my body, I couldn't say, but the pain wasn't unbearable. The walls were a powder blue, which was supposed to be calming and soothing. I could see the dirt and dust and grime covering the blue paint, which lessened the intended effect to near-nonexistence. The doors were uniformly closed and most likely locked; I could tell when we passed from patient to doctor territory by the lack of tray slots at the bottoms of the doors. Jaime's footsteps echoed on the tile floor, bouncing off the walls and into my ears. I couldn't hear anyone else in the hallway; from the sound or lack of it, Jaime and I were the only ones in the building. Logic told me that wasn't the case, but logic doesn't always have all the answers.

My internal voice was telling me to shuffle a bit so I seemed more out of it than I actually was. That made sense, though I had no idea why it made sense. I felt the need to move faster, to get to the answers I knew were all around me. Colors actually seemed brighter, which told me the drugs were more out of my system than before, which added to my sense of hurry. Someone wanted me stoned to the gills, passive and pacified. I had no idea who would want to do so, or even why. In the game of memory, I was missing three-quarters of the pieces, and the last quarter seemed designed by an LSD-laden madman with a morbid sense of humor.

Nevertheless, I kept my head down, trying to act as deflated and defeated as I could remember I was the day before. The voice told me not to overdo it, that there was more going on than met the eye. I mentally shot back a "No shit" before catching myself. The voice gave an approving chuckle rather than the vicious mental smack I expected. Apparently it liked when I stood up to authority. I wasn't sure how I felt about that, but I had little time to think about it as I arrived at the office of Doctor James Odentson, head of the institution and, now that I could think clearly, the only doctor in the entire place.

It was the epitome of a well-learned and well-heeled doctor's office, with bookshelves lining the walls, filled with heavy, thick tomes that only someone who spent most of their life in school to delve into the labyrinth of the human mind would appreciate. Diplomas, framed in wood and glass, showed just how well-learned Odentson was, with a magna cum laude degree from Harvard Medical School alongside a certificate from the Norwegian University of Science. Various other pieces of paper and sheepskin dotted the wood paneling, showing visitors just how amazingly smart and well-qualified the good doctor was. His desk was enormous, tidy and organized. Papers were in a tight pile on the right side of the wooden edifice he sat behind, while folders formed a column on the left.

Behind the desk sat the good doctor, fingers steepled. The chair was an oaken throne with what looked like satin cushions on the back; it didn't take much to guess that similar cushions separated him from the wood. His eyes ticked back and forth across the desk over his fingers, seeming to focus on different spots of the office, then shot up to look at me standing at the open door. A smile formed on his face the moment he saw me, and he rose in one languid motion.

"Ah, there you are, Thomas!" The doctor lifted up a folder from the top of the pile on the left side of his desk. It was at least an inch thick, packed tightly with what I figured was my entire life, or as much of it as was relevant to my reasons for being in the institution. "I almost thought you weren't going to come."

I forced a smile, keeping it somewhat sickly. "It's not like I had a choice." I nodded my head to Jaime. "He's a hard man to ignore."

That got a rumbling chuckle from behind me, and the doctor gestured to the overstuffed chair in front of his desk. "Go ahead and have a seat, Thomas. We have a lot to talk about."

"I bet," I muttered as I sank into the chair, the upholstery ugly but the piece of furniture comfortable beyond belief. A sigh involuntarily escaped my lips as I let the chair engulf me, my hands falling into my lap. My head dropped a bit, though I kept the doctor and Jaime in my sight as best I could.

"Making yourself comfortable, I see. Good!" Doctor Odentson said as he gave a nod to Jaime. I heard the door close and the tread of a gigantic man fade away. My senses were sharper than before, which made it more difficult to pretend to be out of sorts. Of course, the voice in my head still wasn't telling me why I needed to pretend, but everyone has secrets; I would find out sooner or later. "Where to begin with you, Thomas?"

A truism spoke up from the cavernous dark of my memory. To tell the best lie, tell the truth only as far as you have to. That way, you're not technically lying, and technically correct is the best kind of correct. So I did. "I don't remember much, Doc. I don't remember why I'm here. I don't even remember how I got here."

Doctor Odentson pursed his lips and gave a low whistle. "That does make things a bit difficult. For me, I mean." He handed me the folder. "Open it, Thomas."

"What's in it?"

The doctor smiled humorlessly. "Evidence."

I didn't need him to clarify what kind of evidence. Given the bits and pieces I learned after I woke up in the Chair, the good doctor likely put everything against me in my hands. I began to open the manila folder, but was stopped by a hand on mine.

"Are you sure you're ready for this?" Odentson looked concerned, though his eyes glittered somewhat through a trick of the light. "This won't be pleasant."

I pulled the folder and my hands away. "I need to know the truth, Doctor." The folder opened, and I nearly slammed it back shut. As it was, another voice started sounding in my head, this one doing nothing but gibbering at the sights my eyes devoured.

The first thing I saw upon opening the folder was the back of someone's head. It would have been okay if the gaping hole wasn't there, and I could see into the dead man's skull. The picture was in bright color, looking like a production still more than anything else. I could see the pinkish-grey matter inside the wound, along with flecks of white I assumed was bone, and a spatter of purplish-red, no doubt blood. My stomach churned from the sight, threatening to reverse gears, even though it was as empty as a politician's promise.

I turned the picture over and came to the next picture; there was apparently an entire set devoted to a man getting a bullet through his head. Going through each photograph was excruciating, but I knew I had to see them. I needed data, and this was the closest thing I had to it.

"Not pretty, is it?" Odentson mused. When I didn't answer since I was too busy studying a picture of what looked like me wearing a pair of blue jeans and a white shirt, he continued. "These were taken just after the police found you standing over the body. The gun was in your hand, and you were, according to them, raving about the end of the world and how 'they' must be stopped."

"I killed him?" I asked both the doctor and myself.

"There's a picture of you in there with a gun in your hand. You tell me."

"They who?" I still didn't look up. "Who's this 'they' that told me to kill him?"

"You were never clear on that with the police, or even me."

I looked up from the file folder, gauging my next question carefully. "How long have I been here?"

"You've been here a good while, Thomas," the doctor said, "and you will be here as long as it takes to make you well again."

I skipped the monochrome versions of the pictures; they were just repeats, and I had all I could do to keep the whining new voice in my head from squealing and squalling out of control. Moving the pictures out of the way revealed a police report, typed clearly so anyone with working eyes could read.

"Yes, the written word," Odentson smiled, his voice soothing. "That's much more interesting than a bunch of pictures. Your mother said you enjoyed reading. Is that how you got the idea?"

"What idea?" I was only half-listening as I was skimming the report, picking up words and phrases. The first voice, the one that I had been afraid of before, gave a gruff sound of approval at my actions. Absorb the data now, it said, and analyze it later.

"The gods, of course." Odentson laughed quietly. "What a concept!"

"Of course," I agreed, barely caring what he said. The report said the gun was a Colt 1911, chambered in .45 caliber, and I had been only two feet away from the victim, a man named Martin Blackston, when I pulled the trigger. Bells rang when I read the name, but I ignored them in the quest for information.

"Do you know what you did before you came here, Thomas?"

Still not paying much attention, I said, "Shot someone in the head."

The disapproving tone was almost physical. "Before that." When I shook my head, the doctor said, "You told everyone you were a protector of the innocent and weak mortals from the gods." Odentson went behind his desk and sat down. "You would follow people around, convinced they were in some massive conspiracy to bring about the end of the world. This was when you weren't working as a bagger at a supermarket." I looked up again at that. "Yes, Thomas, you suffered from delusions of grandeur the likes have never been seen by anyone in the community. You were the one who would save mortals from the likes of the gods." He let out a smothered chuckle. "You definitely protected those who were preyed upon by the more lustful deities."

His medical manner left something to be desired, but considering what I was reading, especially in the interrogation and confession parts of the file, it made a fair amount of sense. There were a double-dozen orders of protection against me, all granted within the same month. Transcripts of 911 calls featuring women and men claiming someone was standing outside watching their house or apartment. Arrests for assault on those I had apparently thought were attacking the people I was protecting. No trespassing orders for restaurants, stores, malls, four places of worship, and for some strange reason a retirement home. I had definitely been busy.

"The things you said and did brought you here, Thomas. More than anything, it was your outburst that made sure it happened."

I went back to two pictures in particular, this time getting their matching black and white versions. Something was nagging me about them, and I couldn't explain it. There was something off about the way the pictures were.

After I had spent several minutes committing a picture of the entrance wound and the picture of me standing near the body holding a small pistol to memory, I closed the folder. I stood just long enough to put it on the doctor's desk, then sank back with a grateful sigh in the chair. George had done some kind of miracle with his hands, but I still felt a bit pained when moving too much. "What happened to me?"

"You truly don't remember? Well, when you were found not guilty by reason of insanity thanks to me, you went haywire, telling the judge you would bring the sky down on her, the jury, anyone who got in your way."

"That sounds pretty serious, Doc." I pushed against the back of the chair, feeling my spine stretch.

"It was. I was the expert witness who kept you from going to jail for the rest of your life. You should thank me."

"I'll thank you when you cure me. What do I have to do?"

The doctor sat back slowly, folding his hands over his stomach "You have to admit that what you did was wrong. That's the first step."

"That's the thing, Doc: I don't know if I did this."

A disgusted sigh exploded from Odentson as he leaned forward again on his desk. "What do you think? The great conspiracy in your mind has you locked in a mental institution for fun and games? You think you are so special that some great secret ruling body that doesn't exist, run by beings that do not exist, have singled you out to make you their nemesis?" The doctor slapped his hand on the desk. "You've no idea just how insane that sounds, Thomas."

I shrugged my shoulders, lowering my head in submission. In truth, I wanted to get somewhere to think all this information through, and I would not likely get out before at least pretending to admit I had committed such a heinous crime. "You know what insanity looks like, Doctor. You would know best."

James Odentson nodded briskly, a smile forming on his face. "Yes, I would, and this is not actual insanity. You know what happened. Once you admit it to yourself, we can move on to other things and discover more ways you're broken, and the best ways to fix you."

Oh no, that wasn't ominous at all, came the voice in my head. "So I'm not crazy?"

The doctor sat back in his chair, the smile staying in place. "We don't like to use the word 'crazy', especially in your case. 'Confused' would be a better choice."

That was more accurate than he knew. I was more confused about my whole situation than I was before. Getting an idea, I started rubbing the left side of my head at the temple. "I don't feel so good, Doc." I bent over the file folder somewhat, letting out a little moan.

"Oh, dear," he said with what sounded like genuine worry. "Your headaches again. This must have been too much for you to handle at the moment. I'll have Jaime get you back to your room."

I nodded and watched the doctor move swiftly to the office door. Of their own accord, my hands pulled out several of the pictures and a few pages of my file and shove them up my sweatshirt. For later, the voice said. You're going to need them.

I asked the voice, Keep pressure against my stomach to keep the papers from falling out, right?

Pure approval shone through. You're learning. Good. It won't be long.

I didn't have time to ask the obvious follow-up question as Jaime lumbered into the room. Keeping one hand on my stomach and the papers underneath my shirt, I lurched to my feet, my free hand on the chair's arm. I shuffled past Jaime and through the office door, trying to keep my secret cargo from dropping all over the floor. It was hard going, and I thought I was going to slip up, but I managed not to let anything drop.

Once we got back to my room and Jaime went to get me some pills, I lifted my mattress. Thin thing it was, it flew off the bedframe. Before I deposited the pictures and pages, I saw a bit of paper caught in the metal frame. I knew I didn't have time to investigate it, so I filed it away in my head while putting the evidence against me down on the metal springs, then covering it with my hastily retrieved mattress. By the time Jaime got back, I was sitting on the side of my bed, head down, and breathing normally.

"Here you go, Tommy," Jaime's voice boomed, I'm sure unintentionally. "These will make you feel better."

I nodded my thanks and took the proffered plastic shot glass of pills and cup of water. Palming the pills was easy; they dropped harmlessly into the sleeve of my sweatshirt. The water went down easy with two swallows, even with the slightly metallic tang in it. My head immediately started to feel fuzzy.

Oh crap. The water.

I handed back the plastic and patiently waited for Jaime to leave. Once he did, I went to the toilet and shoved a finger into the back of my throat. The result was quick and expected. My mental passenger and co-pilot notified me I likely didn't get all the drugged water out, but enough to not feel the full effects.

As I lay there on the floor, kneeling against the bowl with my forehead on the cool porcelain, I heard footsteps, then my door opening. Wearily, I turned to look who was coming to visit.

"Well, you figured it out," George said, a smile on his dark face. "Good job."

"What do they drug the water for?"

"Docility. It works pretty well when you aren't expecting it." George helped me to my feet. I held onto him, and his robe was soft and rather comforting. "Of course, when you are expecting it, you need to know how to get out of drinking it." He sat me on the bed and reached into a pocket, pulling out a small metal cup, an iron nail and a Zippo lighter. "The drugs don't react well to heat. Fire up the lighter, heat up the nail, drop it into the cup. Wait about three minutes and it's drinkable. The water, I mean."

"Why are you helping me?" Finding out I was being drugged at every turn was doing wonders for my trust issues.

"As I said before, I'm helping you because you're helping yourself, Tom." He began digging through my dresser drawers before tossing me the robe he found. "Use this to hide what I gave you. They'll take it in a heartbeat if they find it." I did as he asked, putting the items in a pocket. "Good. Now for the real reason I came over. Now comes the real fun."

I gave George a sideways glance. "Fun?"

"Off your ass and on your feet, Thomas Statford." George cracked his knuckles and smiled. "It's training day."

Chapter Seven

I collapsed in the middle of my fourth set of pushups.

Okay, so collapsed isn't the right word. However, it's the best I can come up with to describe the event without resorting to simply saying my arms gave out and my face hit the freezing concrete floor. And yes, it hurt.

George had led me through the halls of the institution to what looked like an abandoned part of the building. From what I could see, it had been months since someone had been there; as the dust was thick and undisturbed. The room had taken over an hour to clean, mainly because I was the only one cleaning. George leaned against the wall, advice and clean rags the only offerings of help. By the time I was done, I could see out through the windows. It was a pointless exercise, as there was a blizzard currently bellowing around the building.

The room might have been a conference room at one time, but the table and chairs were long gone. There were drawings on the walls, mostly graphs and charts, but there were words as well. "Synergy" and "consensus" were scrawled along with other corporate buzzwords in various colors, faded with time. It was about fifty paces long by twenty paces wide. I knew this because George had me measure it out before he started me running sprints back and forth, one wall to the other, then back again.

After sprints came the pushups. Then more running. Then there were more pushups. After that, to add a bit of variety came more running. I don't mind saying I was quite a bit winded after the second round of sprints, but George was implacable.

"Come on, man!" George bellowed in my ear. I tried ignoring him and just enjoying the cool stone against my burning sweating face and chest. My sweatshirt had been taken off after the first set of sprints. It was on the floor somewhere, though I was a bit more concerned with completing my sets than my shirt. "You think Ira is going to let you fall over like that and take a rest when he's beating you to death?" The memories of Ira pummeling me were still fresh in my mind, but I felt myself drifting away. George squatted down next to me. My left eye rolled up at him and saw the disgust on his face. "You think this is a game? He will kill you, and likely not think anything more of you after washing your blood off his fists. The last part of you will go down a drain, and no one will care."

That was a pretty grisly incentive to get up. It worked. My arms pushed my body up to the ready position, and I continued my exercises. By the time I was done, I could barely feel my limbs.

George tossed me a towel, which landed on my head as I couldn't get my hand up in time to catch it. "Not bad for a start. You still need to work on your endurance, but your strength is there."

I managed to get the towel off my face and started rubbing my chest clear of sweat and dirt. "I hate to break it to you, man, but I'm not Ralph Macchio." I chuckled. "And you're a bit too tall for Mr. Miyagi."

The ebony man clapped his hands together and laughed . "You have no idea." He bent over and grabbed my sweatshirt, flicking it out to pop the dust off it. "Here, Daniel-san. When you snatch sweatshirt from hand, you will be ready," he intoned in his best Miyagi voice.

"That was terrible." I took the shirt and slipped it on. My arms were getting their feeling back, which was good for me.

"Yeah, George, that was really naughty of you," came a husky voice from the conference room's doorway.

George grumbled in barely concealed disgust, and I understood why; both he and I recognized the voice as Milton. And where one was, the other….

"Absolutely disgusting, George. Let me in, Milt. I wanna see." Oh yeah. Not far behind at all.

"They aren't doing anything, Dante." Milton moved his considerable bulk into the room anyway, allowing Dante entrance. "Not anymore, anyway."

I felt energy surging into my arms and legs. Power, born of anger. The leering on Milton's face was evident, and the innuendo couldn't have been clearer if he had shouted it into a megaphone. My hands balled into fists, the leaden quality gone. I felt my legs begin to tremble as they bent in preparation to leap onto Milton and do some facial rearrangement.

It was my first time seeing these two, though not my first time meeting them; that was the night before after my body was used as a side of beef by a psychotic Rocky Balboa. They were almost mirror images of each other, the only exceptions being Milton having coal-colored hair and a pencil-thin moustache, and Dante having red hair cut in a spiky style. Both men were about as big as

Jaime, and nearly as wide. I use the term "men" loosely, as calling them fucksticks was not much for polite conversation. On these two, their girth looked to be more fat than muscle, but appearances can be deceiving.

A hand on my shoulder stopped me, draining the anger from me. "It was nothing like that, Milton," George said, his tone even. "It was nothing like that and you know it."

Milton shrugged his shoulders, a gesture one of superiority graciously bestowed upon us lower life forms. "Ah, we were hoping. Better than most of the crap we see around here."

"You disgust me, Milton." George's eyes darted to Dante, who had entered the room and was leaning against the wall. "And your little minion, too."

"Blow it out your ass. We don't answer to you. You're lucky we don't tell the doc about you two." The orderly seemed actually taken aback by the words before regaining his sense of authority.

George's mouth hooked into Cheshire grin, showing perfectly straight, white teeth. "Oh, please do tell him. Perhaps he could ask the both of you about Ellen's constant regression into her ways. I'm sure he's curious as to how you two always seem to be around when she has her eh hmm ---" he paused, clearing his throat, "moments of weakness."

That shut Milton down instantly. His mental chubby of getting us in Dutch with the doctor visibly deflated. "Fine. Fuck it. Get back to the main wing. You're not supposed to be here, especially with that guy," he spouted, pointing at me.

"We'll go where we please, Milton. You cannot stop us. "

With that, George led the way past Dante and Milton. I could feel the seething anger from the two orderlies emanating as I side-walked between them. Their beady little eyes followed us as we made our way back to the central building of the institution. George set a swift pace, The energy in my legs was gone like smoke in a hurricane. I struggled to keep up with him.

"You don't like them much, do you?" I said to try and get George to slow a bit.

It didn't work.

"Not really. They started here a couple of months ago, and have been working the night shift like it's their own personal kingdom." George's head turned slightly toward me. "And brothel."

I started to slow down, but sped up to keep pace. "And Doctor Odentson doesn't stop them?"

This time, George did slow down. I saw we had made it to the main building. "The good doctor believes in a hands-off approach to therapy. Part of the rules here."

"That makes no sense! How are we supposed to get well?"

George stopped at that, and turned to look at me. The expression he wore was incredulous. "Get well?" He mused. "What makes you think anyone in this place wants to get better?" He turned away and resumed his pace.

Some light of understanding dawned on me. "So the inmates run the asylum."

"Not exactly. You could say we have a mutual understanding. At least we used to." George seemed to almost fume in anger. "The additions of Dante and Milton changed the dynamic quite a bit."

"I don't like them very much."

"You aren't the only one. However, the rules say that those in the white coats are in charge, so we follow what they say, for the most part."

We arrived back at my room, where I changed into clean clothes. Still sweatpants and a sweatshirt, still blue, but they were clean, at least for the moment. I needed a shower badly, and said as much to George.

"It should be safe. I don't think Ira will be let out of solitary for another day or two." George laughed. "He may be a battering lunatic, but he obeys the law and the letter. You still have six days."

I painted a plastic smile on my face. "You have no idea how that fills me with confidence."

"Just get cleaned up. It's nearly suppertime." George left, leaving me to head to the communal showers.

I pushed down the uneasy feeling of going somewhere alone. The showers were segregated by gender, which was fine by me. I stripped down, goosebumps forming in the chill air. The tile was cold as I stepped in. I turned on the middle of five spigots. The water was ice.. After a few minutes, it warmed up and I felt my muscles unknot from the steaming water hitting them.

My body was a roadmap of scar tissue. Each nick, scrape, and lesion painted a picture of what I could only guess my life was before this place. The pucker on my left thigh told me something pierced deep into my flesh. The slivers of impressions on both sides of my ribcage spoke of a fight with a clawed something. Whatever it was, it was big, bad, and exceptionally pissed off at me. The water rained down on me, I relished in its warmth scrubbing off the dirt and sweat and dust. I looked at the jagged tears of skin around my wrists; when something in my head clicked.

"Those aren't suicidal marks, are they?" I asked the voice in my head. When it did not answer, I felt I was on the right track. I traced a scar on my head that had been revealed by the shaving of my hair. My fingers went bumping over the ghost of a wound. There were other scars on my head, but that one was the biggest and, the most recent from what I could tell.

I was getting the feeling that nothing was as it seemed, least of all me. Things were beginning to add up, but not computing like they were supposed to. It was more like algebra rather than basic math; my brain was missing several variables. I was locked in an asylum for the insane, psychotic, and violent, with no way out; what was more, at least one of the locals had me on their hit list making things a touch more difficult.

"Well, if it isn't the only real nutball in this shithole!"

The woman's voice bounced off the tiles, shocking me out of my thoughts and back to what barely passed for reality. I instinctively covered myself with one hand while trying to clear my eyes of water and reach for my towel with the other. The most I did was the first part, which didn't improve things very much, considering what and who I saw.

Lucy, her red hair was flowing free, covering her ears and framing a pale freckle free face with her hands on her hips, her jaw jutting forward in a way that screamed arrogance, stood at the entrance. I hated that look; it was the audacity of arrogance, like the whole world was intruding on her, robbing her of proper recognition of her superiority. If I didn't know better, I thought she had visited a beauty shop or hair salon in the last day. She was clothed in the usual garb of patients, but tight on her, conforming to every curve. It would have been a bit fetching if she weren't looking down her nose at the entire universe.

Standing next to her was a red-faced beast of a young man. The presence of anger and hatred in his features made me take a step back; he was like a redneck on steroids and moonshine and I had a lit match to the confederate flag. . The steam from the shower was nothing compared to the smoke that exploded from his ears. He was taller than Lucy by a full head, his hands closing into fists the size of roasts at the end of arms double packed with muscle. Sweat covered his bald head, the pores squeezing out moisture from the heat. This monster, my brain reminded me, was Ira. He definitely looked different when I had two functioning eyes.

Thinking about it, I should have known it was a bad idea to go anywhere, much less the showers, by myself, but we all have our roles to play. I knew for a fact if I went to clean up, I would likely be attacked. Moreover, I knew if I was attacked someone would get hurt, and hurt badly. Things were starting to filter into my head, filling the holes in my Swiss cheese memory. Someone, most likely me, was going to get hurt.

"Heard you were talking shit about Ira," Lucy sneered.

I kept silent, gauging my chances to escape as somewhere between no way and not a snowball's chance in hell.

What can I say? I'm nothing if not an optimist.

"Talking about me ain't a good idea, meat." Ira started to enter the showers, but was held back by Lucy's hand on his chest. "I'm going to rip your fucking spleen out."

"I didn't say anything to anyone," I said, trying to keep a low non-threatening tone. "I was unconscious most of the night, I couldn't have said anything, remember? After all, you're the one who made that happen."

"And I'll make it happen again. You scared, meat?" Ira pushed against Lucy's hand. She enjoyed having that kind of power over someone, and seemed overly proud of herself for keeping Ira at bay. The look on her face was pure glee.

One of the things I was discovering about myself was I didn't deal well with blustering bullies, and this guy was one of the worst. "Should I be?"

That brought him up short, but only for a moment. A vulpine smile formed and I thought he licked his lips. "You're lucky she's here and you got time, you little smartass." Ira pushed away from her and straightened to his full height. I had to crane my neck up to look at him, and I felt my resolve start to fall apart like a barn in a tornado.

Dammit, why did the guys I have to fight have to be built like brick shithouses?

Wait. Who had I been fighting? I had never been in a fight before in my life. The more I thought about it, the more I could feel the lie in it. I had been in fights before; the atlas of scars exposed the truth. They had apparently been terrible, colossal battles, starting on a cataclysmic level and escalating up to the what the unholy fuck scale.

My knees started to shake and I was about to cower under Ira's murderous gaze before I realized something. I survived. I had been through a lot of terrible things, and lived to tell about it; if I could remember them, but nonetheless I survived.

The thought filled me with the confidence I needed. . "Time is on my side, Ira." I formed a smile and brought my eyes up to meet his, new strength in my spine. I had power building inside of me, and it wanted out. "We'll see what happens when I'm ready for you. See how good you are when you aren't beating on a defenseless man. I might surprise you."

That almost set him off. "I will eat your heart, motherfucker!" This time, Lucy had to hold him back with both hands, screaming into his face, getting her own covered by his spittle-flecked threats of what he would do to me the next time we met. I stood my ground, not caring anymore that I was wet, soapy, and naked in front of two strangers. Not a day ago, I would have thought myself unable to even stand up to a child, my self-doubt crippling me into inaction at best. However, in that moment I was, invincible, standing against a violent kill-crazy monster who wanted nothing more than to eat my heart.

Amazing what a lightning bolt will do for you.

Lucy finally got him calmed down enough to get out, giving me her patented look of doom as they left, Ira sputtering and cussing the entire way. I let out a breath I didn't know I was holding and leaned against the sweating tile. My heartrate was somewhere in the triple-digits and I felt pain in my palms from where my fingernails had bitten into them. I hadn't realized how tightly I was holding my hands into fists, but the wounds weren't as bad as I thought they were. The bleeding from the half-moon shapes was already stopping as I put my hands under the spraying water. I hissed at the sudden pain, then watched the blood go from my hands down the drain.

I blinked, and the lights went out. Literally.

They did, leaving me in pitch blackness. My right hand reached for the knobs for the water so I would have something to steady myself. The chrome was warm to the touch, and very slippery, but comforting. The cynic that was in my head figured it was Lucy trying to get back at me for getting Ira riled up. Again, I am a total frigging optimist.

That was before the lights started flickering and I saw the bodies. I screamed. The strobe effect didn't do much for my peace of mind either, as my eyes grabbed details in the light between every sliver of darkness. There were caverns ns in their chests, where their hearts were supposed to be. Blood spurted out in rhythmic jets, each pulse growing weaker and weaker. Streams of red criss-crossed, missing me completely, forming a geometric prison around me. .

The body nearest me was a man in some kind of open robe garnished with green feathers and sopping up the dark red spatter. I could see the gaping wound where his heart used to be, light reflecting off the ivory shards of his ribcage. His gray hair was spread about his head in a halo, the look of peace on his face seemed so at odds with the utter desecration of his body. I felt both unfathomable hate for him, but also a pity. This was a man in a utopian haze. He was pleased with what happened to him, as if he wanted it to happen.

It was the look of a man in ecstasy.

My hand was still on the water knob, the chrome fixture cutting into my flesh. I knew what I was seeing wasn't real; the carnage was all around me, yet I could still feel the metal in my hand. I stepped back quickly against the tile again, hoping I felt it instead of empty air. The back of my head smacked painfully against the tile, making me see stars. I could feel a darkness pulsing around me, trying to get in, pushing against me and my mind, trying to make me think and see other things that were not me.

I began mumbling gibberish, shutting my eyes against the terrible sight around me. I felt a rhythm to the sounds my mouth made, almost like a language. More sounds and syllables flowed out of me like the water that surrounded me. My voice grew louder, more confident in what I was saying, even though I had no idea what was flowing from my lips. The more my mouth moved, the more I felt safe.

I didn't care what I was saying; with almost-human regret the darkness subsided. My eyes opened slowly, taking in the white tile around me. The light stopped their flickering, with the scene returning to normal from the Bosch landscape I thought I was standing in only seconds before. There was no sign of blood, bodies, or gore. Just me, my hurt hands, and my head throbbing inside and out.

I cursed under my breath as I pulled my aching hand away. Something had happened in there, something completely impossible. I could feel the beginnings of a headache coming on, and it was going to be a bad one. My earlier premonition had come true; I was going to get hurt.

I hate it when I'm right.

Chapter Eight

The water from the ocean tickled my feet as the tide brought the waves in, covering my toes which I dug deep into the sand. It was soft sand, not at all gritty from the constant wash of seawater and I relished the sensation. To my very likely flawed recollection, I had never seen the ocean except in pictures on the television or in magazines. I couldn't care less; this was how I felt a beach should be, and how an ocean should feel. The crash of the waves was soothing, a heartbeat for the world around me. A damned shame it was nothing but a dream.

I was wearing only a pair of swim trunks this time. It was the third night since my first meeting with Ira, and the second time I tried to go back to the dream. I had spent hours the night before trying to get back to the lake, but my mind stubbornly kept me from what I considered a paradise. Sure, it was boring, but to get away from the constant blizzard and the hellish cold, anywhere was preferable.

I'd just have to make sure I watched for any lightning bolts.

There was a scent on the wind, coming from behind me. It was different than the salt of the water. This was a lilting aroma, light and delicate. I knew what flower it was, or thought I did; gardening didn't seem to be part of the knowledge that was slowly filtering back into my fractured memory. It was a white flower. I knew that much, but what kind?

"You're going to drive yourself crazy trying to figure everything out at once," came the woman's voice. She was behind me, as always. I could hear her feet on the sand.

I shook my head at her choice of words. "That just means I'm in the right place. If I'm crazy, they can fix me here."

There was a pause, the only sounds the wind on the water and the waves crashing into the beach. Bare feet rasped on the sand and I heard a sigh from my left. "You know what I mean," she said.

"Of course, I do. I just wanted to be a smartass."

A rueful chuckle sounded from the woman as my ears picked up the sound of her sitting down. "Struck by lightning, gets worked out by a guy in a bathrobe, and stands up to a guy who wants your guts for garters." There was wonder in her words. "Then you try and find me. You certainly are dedicated."

"I wasn't trying to find you," I said, my voice quiet.

"Still a terrible liar, though. Here." There was a bit of movement behind me, then I felt someone behind me, sitting with their back to mine. "You found me. What are you going to do now that you've found me?"

"I want some answers," I heard myself say, but that wasn't true. Not completely true, at least.

"You want answers, Tommy, but do you even know the questions?"

The Zen crap was starting to get on my nerves, but I marked it down to my own subconscious trying to keep me from blowing up my own brain with too much discovery. I was started to figure I wasn't really supposed to be in an asylum. The question, of course, was how to prove it. Not just prove it to the doctor, but to myself.

I would not be a monster.

"Okay, Mystery Lady," I said as my voice filled with equal parts bravado and fear. "What are the rules on the questions?"

There was a chuckle that vibrated into my body from her. I could feel her head shake behind mine. "What makes you think there are rules, Tommy?"

"If there weren't rules, I would have turned around and seen you the first night."

That brought a roar of laughter and a shuddering against my back. "Yes, you're coming along nicely." As I turned to face her and ask what she meant, her voice whip cracked against me. "Don't you dare turn around!" I felt like I gave myself whiplash facing forward. "That's the big rule: Until you're ready to never see me again, you can't turn around."

I sighed loudly, wondering what the big deal was. Still, it was what she wanted, and who was I to refuse her? "Okay, so what other rules do we have for this little interlude, lady?"

"You get five questions tonight, Tommy," she answered. "We might have some time together before the little scrap you're going to have with Ira, but don't count on it."

Pained laughter escaped me. "That's better than I thought I'd get."

"I'll also answer your questions within reason," she continued. "No skipping ahead to the end, especially when you know I won't know the answer."

"What if I already know the answer?"

"Then you wouldn't need two other complete strangers in your head pointing things out to you, and you wouldn't be in this situation in the first place." There was a derisive tone in her voice as she continued. "You also aren't dumb enough to waste your questions on something stupid like that."

I grudgingly allowed the point, though I was starting to get a bit tired of being told what to do, even though I was in my own head. "So the question and answer starts…?"

"Right now."

"Okay, then, here's my first one: Am I actually crazy?"

The answer was immediate. "Big time, but not in the way to get you locked up in a sanitarium." There was a pause, then she chided, "Come on, Tommy. You wasted a question on that? You should know better than that."

"I just wanted to make sure. That I'm not explains a few things, but not why I'm here." That brought another question to mind. "Why am I in a mental institution?"

She took a little longer to answer this one. "For your own good. Believe me, if you weren't here, you would probably be dead."

I slumped forward a bit, crossing my legs so I could sit more comfortably. "Who would have killed me?"

"That's the wrong question, but I'll answer it anyway: everyone who once called you friend and enemy, hero and villain, good guy and bad guy." Her voice took on a singsong rhythm with the last few words. "It didn't matter that it wasn't your fault, even when it was all your fault; they would have wanted blood."

"That's three questions," I muttered to myself. The next two had to count; I didn't want to waste any more chances at gathering data. "What can you tell me about the asylum?"

"There are two things in the entire institution that are not what they appear to be. Everything else is, for better or worse, exactly what they look like."

There was a moment where she didn't say anything, and I couldn't think of anything else I needed to know for the time being. The idea that I was being kept someplace for protection made some sense, but I had to temper the thought with the knowledge I wasn't talking to some other actual being, but a voice in my head that was pretending to be someone else. I had more information than I had before, even with the knowledge I was likely only telling myself things I should have recognized from the moment I woke up.

My mind started working through the things I had been thinking and feeling between the first dream and this one, piecing together the clues I seemed to be giving myself. "I'm seeing things clearer than before, noticing things that no one else should. These feelings are not my own; they're from before, when I wasn't stuck in this place.

"It can't be because of the lack of drugs in my system or the punishment George is putting me through. There are still holes in my memory, things I know I should remember but don't. I can feel them pushing against my mind, wanting to come out." I held my head in my hands, rubbing my temple on the left side. That motion was so much a telltale of an oncoming headache five minutes afterward, I could nearly set a watch by it. Even in a dream, I could feel the oncoming pain, a freight hauler barreling down the straightaway of my mind, bearing down on me, loaded with nothing but agony. "Who am I?"

"You're Thomas Statford. You are who you have always been." I heard her get up, the feel of her back leaving mine. I almost turned to watch her go before I stopped myself. "Don't let anyone tell you otherwise."

"Wait!" I leaned forward on my hands and knees to stand without looking at her. "I didn't want to ask that!"

"Rules are rule, Tommy," she said, her voice tinged with regret. "We'll see each other again. Don't worry about that. Good luck." My ears caught her footsteps rasping in the sand as she walked away from me.

"I'm not. I just don't even know your name." Her steps stopped abruptly. "I mean, you're my dream woman and I don't know who you are."

There was a sigh from behind me, then the footsteps came toward me. I felt soft fingertips on my neck, the touch like ice. There was warmth in the gesture, even if there wasn't in the fingers. "Tommy, my Tommy," she whispered. Sadness covered the words like a shroud. "You really are all alone, aren't you?" I started to say something and she shushed me. "I'll tell you this much: you know me, you know who I am, and you know my name."

"I do? How do I know you?"

"No answers, at least not for now." The caressing fingers retreated, leaving a cold fiery sensation in their sudden absence. "When you do remember who I am, you have to remember one other thing."

I rubbed the back of my neck where she had touched. The sensation of her fingers was still there. "What's that?"

"Say my name and be free." Her voice seemed to be fading, but I hadn't heard her move at all. "When you're ready to go, when you remember, you just have to say my name and you will be free."

"Just like that?" My voice was incredulous but even I could hear the faint twinge of hope in my words. "That's all it takes to be free?"

"Freedom is never without its cost, Tommy." Her voice was a whisper on the surf. "You of all people know that." With that, she vanished.

I didn't bother turning around to verify she was gone; that's the way dreams are. I stared out at the far-off horizon, the sun starting to set on the ocean. The woman and I had not been talking that long, but then I wasn't carrying a watch, and dreamtime can be completely on its own time, with hours seeming like minutes and seconds lasting days. I recalled a movie where people could live lifetimes in their dreams. It had frightened me at the time when, for only a brief moment, I couldn't tell if I were in a dream or awake. Ridiculous, I know, but it had been a very good movie.

The difference in this was I knew I was dreaming. The beach wasn't real, nor was the woman. They were nothing more than places and people from a past I couldn't remember forming a backdrop for my subconscious to act out whatever happened to be in my brain. With a thought, I could make the world around me vanish; I had no such power over the institution, much as I wanted otherwise.

The answers the woman gave me gave me some hope, even considering their source. It didn't change the reality of my situation, which was locked up in a looney bin, but it put some things in perspective. If I wasn't crazy, or the type of crazy that needed being under lock and key, that meant the thoughts and feelings I had before that first dream were not really mine. Someone wanted me pliant and suggestible and essentially useless. Whoever wanted that was an asshole.

Thinking about the people in the institution, I was discovering I was surrounded by assholes.

Since I was alone, I made the pictures I had stolen from the file appear. I had memorized every single line and color of them, and being able to conjure the photos up in my head was a pretty neat trick. The mental imagery kept me from having to constantly watch for Jaime or the Doublemint Twins while I studied the pictures. As I also didn't need any more distractions, I made the beach into a small room, no windows or doors, no decorations on the walls. Just a table and chair occupied the room, and I used them, sitting down and spreading the pictures out so I could look at them carefully.

With a wave of my hand, I conjured up the police report, or at least the pages I had taken from my file. I hadn't had time to be picky. Some of the words were fuzzy to my recollection, so they were distorted on the page in front of me. I leaned forward onto my elbows, focusing on the words that were clear. Words like "close range" and "large-caliber" jumped out at me, painting a picture for me of what brought me to the Twin Friezes Institute for Mental Health.

Or to be more accurate, what supposedly brought me there.

Being in a dream world is better than being in the real world sometimes, at least when it comes to reconstructing a crime scene. With a thought, I made the scene of the execution appear, at least as far as I knew. It was very barebones with no scenery, but anything not directly related to the crime was useless to me. Scenery didn't matter; the scenario did.

I was standing behind Blackston, who was on his knees. I was wearing a white shirt and jeans, while the victim wore a suit of some kind. The gun, which didn't seem to fit properly in my hand because it was both too big and too small, oscillated between a foot from his head and right against it. My mind was working overtime on all the possible variables, trying to make the event fit the evidence. It was a frozen moment in time, and I could see why I had been fingered as the killer.

The problem was, given what I knew, the whole thing made no sense.

There were some details missing, and I needed those before I could continue. I was running out of time, though. Saturday was coming and I doubted Ira would grant me a reprieve just because I was trying to prove my innocence. In fact, that would likely just urge him to destroy me even more. Altruism didn't seem high in his list of virtues.

Regardless, I needed more data. I needed particulars. I wasn't going to get them in dreams. I wouldn't find the facts locked up in some dark recess of the black hole that was my brain. The only place I would find anything was the real world.

With a disgusted gesture, I destroyed everything around me, sending it back into the ether. The evidence didn't fit the facts and vice versa. I allowed myself to ascend back up the layers of consciousness, back to what passed for the real world. I had questions needing answers, and the only person who had those answers was a certain doctor who had a vested interest in me. Not necessarily my case, but in me.

I felt myself fill out my body, and saw dim light through my closed eyelids. I opened them to the rough ceiling of my cell. There was no denying it to myself anymore. I was a prisoner. I was more likely to be carried out than walk out.

Still, the woman's words drifted up from my thoughts. "Say my name and be free," she had whispered. I couldn't leave, though.

Not yet. Not without knowing what was done to me, and what I had

supposedly done.

I had to know.

Chapter Nine

Time flowed as it always does, going from moment to moment, hour to hour, day to day. At least that was how it was supposed to do. In actuality, it sped up and slowed down in an almost madcap state, like a movie projector with a faulty motor. Two days passed without incident, or as much as anything like living in a madhouse could pass without incident. I ate the horrid meals they fed me, heated my water so I wouldn't go into a drugged stupor, and George trained the hell out of me. There were times I would do little more than crawl back to my bunk and pass out, resting fitfully for an hour or two before waking to George returning for my training, or more therapy.

After a time, I almost looked forward to seeing Jaime rather than George. At least when the doctor tortured me, I was able to sit down for it.

The therapy sessions were intense, almost to the point of interrogations. On the third day, the doctor stood up and walked behind where I sat. I could feel his presence behind me, his measured breathing much deeper than normal. He seemed to be getting frustrated. "You stood behind him, Thomas!" he shouted at me. "Stay Still!" He nudged when I turned to look. "Your victim couldn't look at you! Why should you get that courtesy? That privilege?" Odentson twisted the word, giving it a sarcastic tone. "Look at that report. What does it say?"

I picked up the paper and read it, my eyes scanning the words, trying to piece together just exactly how this was possible.

There was a hard nudge to the back of my head. "Read it aloud."

"'I told him not to look at me, and to be happy,'" I said, the words monotone. "'I said he was going to be an instrument of the gods, and his death would make things better for everyone.'" I put the paper down, not believing a word of it. I wasn't even reading what was there. I was skipping ahead, reading and memorizing the various details that were missing from my mental pictures. I needed more data, and I was getting it, even if the price was being in the same room as the not-so-good Doctor Odentson. My mind wasn't analyzing the information. It was storing it as snapshots for later use. That was fine, though. I had all I needed.

Another jab to the back of my head brought me back to reality, this time where my skull had bounced off the concrete. That brought a wince of pain. "Do you remember doing that, Thomas?" He shoved my head harder, when I shook my head. "It says it right there you admitted to it." He screamed in my ear with another jolt to my head. "That says you proudly told the police you made another human being get on their knees in front of you." Jab. "Like a prisoner of war to be executed." Jab. "So you wouldn't have to look into their eyes when you shot them." Jab. Every other word brought a shove to the back of my head. It was getting very old, very quickly.

"I don't remember doing it, Doc!" I spat the words, my head turning again toward my tormentor.

Odentson smacked the back of my head, harder than before, making my ears ring. "It says right there this is what you did, Thomas. Right there!"

"I don't care what it says!" My temper was starting to slip its reigns. "Stop hitting me!"

He smacked me again anyway. "Is this something you think you could do?" Another smack. "Could you just blatantly execute someone like this?"

I felt his hand coming for another hit, and I leaned forward. Twisting around bringing me face to face with the good doctor, who seemed to be smiling. I grabbed him by the wrist and slammed it down on the back of the leather chair. I pulled him close to me by the lapels of his coat. The smile vanished in an instant as I held him no more than an inch away from me. "No, you stone-brained son of a bitch, I wouldn't."

We stayed like that for a plastic moment, nearly nose to nose. I could smell the aftershave Odentson used, cloying in my nostrils, along with the undertone of some other scent. My mind associated it with Christmas, for some reason. I ignored it and pointedly let him go, turning my back to the man again. After a minute, Odentson returned to his place in front of me, straightening his lapels and looking very grim.

"That was uncalled for, Thomas," he said, his voice tight. "I pushed a bit, but you actually hurt me." I tried not to say anything, but apparently my face was screaming into a megaphone. "I think you need a day or two by yourself to ponder your actions."

He called for Jaime, who came in quickly, grabbing my arms with practiced ease. I struggled against him, feeling his hands tighten around my biceps. "Let me go, dammit!" I shouted, trying to pull my arms from his hands. I might as well have been trying to move the earth with a pushup. "This is bullshit!"

"Thomas, you had no reason to touch me. You're starting to regress into what brought you here in the first place. We can't have that," Odentson concluded, pulling out a small syringe. I fought harder, not wanting any more artificial sleep in my system. There was likely some in the slop we were given as food, but not enough to make a difference. That crap I could fight off easily with enough exercise and movement. The stuff in that syringe, however, was a cannon of sleep blasted straight into my head. I could walk to Timbuktu and back and still not have it out of my system.

With a needle in my arm all the fight drained out of me. I felt the stick, jagged pain followed by liquid cold, spreading like mercury over a windowpane. My mind retreated from the onslaught of nothingness, trying to stay pure, trying to stay awake. It was trying like mad to keep the information I gained from disappearing. Dimly, out of the corner of my awareness, I saw the floor go by, the herringbone pattern on the carpet looking ridiculous as it twisted and turned. I knew I was seeing things, and the carpet wasn't moving, that it was my perceptions that were moving. It helped some, but I could feel the fatty piece of beef I had eaten for lunch start to roil in my stomach. I wasn't going to fight the inevitable, and pulled Jaime to the nearest bathroom I could see on our way. He was at least kind enough to let me empty out in a sink rather than spilling all over.

Once Jaime wiped my mouth off, I was taken to the hole. Solitary confinement. It was a place I had only heard about but never seen, and never wanted to see, considering who else made their home there. The door was thick metal, wrought iron if my addled brain was any judge, and at least three inches thick. I had time to wonder what the hell they were keeping down there that needed three inch iron doors before retching again. Thankfully it was only a dry heave and I saw I was about to go into a windowless, lightless room. The walls were metal as well, though they seemed gouged with long lines, almost like claw marks. They were shallow grooves, but even I knew anything that could damage iron like that had to be immensely strong and terribly sharp. That did nothing for my peace of mind. Nothing at all.

Jaime set me down on the thin mat on the floor. His manner was gentle, not letting my head thump on the mat, which really offered no protection from the cold of the stone. I curled into a ball, my hands covering my cramping stomach. Jaime looked down on me from what seemed a thousand miles up. "I'm sorry, Tommy," he said, his voice actually sounding full of sorrow. "You should have known not to touch the doc. He's fussy about that." He squatted down and whispered, "They promised he wouldn't get touched, but don't tell anyone I told you that."

He stood slowly, a mountain on legs. "It's going to be okay, though. He thinks this might be the breakthrough you need. Get some sleep, though; you're going to need it. He'll be down to look in on you soon." In the dim light, I saw Jaime smile. "I'll keep an eye on you, too. Don't worry, Tommy. All will be well."

The door closed, the clank of metal against metal giving the gesture a finality that sank my heart. There was no light source in the room save for a thin line at the bottom of the door, barely a quarter of an inch, and I could barely see anything on the other side of it. All else around me was pure blackness. There could have been pictures of the Superfriends wearing thongs painted on the walls and I would have no idea. I might as well have been thrown in the bottom of a well at midnight after being blindfolded.

I closed my eyes as another pang of nausea hit me, making me curl up into a ball even more. It was likely the fact I had been relatively clean of the drugs that made this dose hit me so hard. The taste of vomit was still in my mouth, the bile burning the underside of my tongue. My muscles relaxed and tightened at random, making me seem to feel like I was having a very slow seizure. I could barely turn to lay on my back, which didn't really matter to me. If I could breathe, I still had the opportunity to learn a few things. For the moment, though, I needed to just let things run their course and have my body come back from the drugs coursing through my veins. Even with the phenobarbital or whatever it was that was shot into me, I could feel the onset of another headache. This one would be a whopper, one that would have me wanting to pull my own head off to make the pain stop. There was one thing I could do, which would help. It was the only thing I could do.

One part of my brain I set to start counting, and to bring me up when it hit five thousand. The rest was where I would do some more almost-literal soul-searching. I had the information locked in my head, and there was little chance of me forgetting it. All that remained was to see just where everything fit together and who was doing what to me.

Something told me I wouldn't have far to look.

Once my counter started, I dove into my own mind, past the oncoming dagger of pain of my headache. As I sank below the depths of consciousness, I wondered what those headaches were. They had no rhyme or reason, and seemed to happen when I was under stress or threatened. I amended that when I remembered I didn't get any headaches when Ira showed up at the shower with Lucy, and that was definitely threatening and stressful.

I pushed away the thoughts and concerns about my head as I came to a landing in a dark corner of my brain, the only place that felt untouched by the drug Odentson had put in me. The visualization helped me a bit to keep myself on the level, but I knew I was in a lot of trouble. The count I gave myself was good for about an hour and a half or less. By then the drugs would be on their way out of my system, and I could get to work in earnest.

For the moment, though, all I could really do is get the information categorized. I pictured a filing cabinet with the word "Evidence" on it. I opened it and started filing everything I had learned from my looking through Odentson's folder. Pictures went in one file, words went into another.

I knew my time was limited. It wasn't likely anyone would be able to resist me being in solitary and want to get a bit of practice on beating my ass. Ira was likely in the cell next to me, but I had no worries about him. As I filed, I threw a mental bulletin board up to hang in the air, showing me all the possible dangers I had to deal with. Removing possible overdose on barbiturates and slipping on wet tiles in the shower as dangers, I focused on the people.

Ira was top of the list, though I didn't think him likely as a danger before Saturday. He wanted me, not just dead, but utterly annihilate. That much rage wrapped up in one person was insane, but at least he was in the right place. He was not a real danger as Lucy had been able to hold him back with a gesture. Either she possessed powers and abilities far beyond mere mortals, or Ira was bound to wait.

That led me to another thought: who or what was holding Ira's leash? That monster could have ended me in that shower, or even in the basement where I first made the beast's acquaintance. Someone wanted me around in top form, and someone wanted him to be the one who ended me. There was a game going on behind the scenes, and it was apparently very important that I remain alive.

My suspect list whittled away until I got to four people. Milton, Dante, Lucy, and the doctor. The more I considered it, the more Doctor Odentson made sense as the one in charge, in more ways than one. The inmates were under his complete control, even the ones who talked back to him in pure open defiance. I had no doubt that Ira could tear Odentson apart, and if the other inmates decided to get involved, the doctor would be toast. Odentson had control over them. The question was why did he have control over them, and how did I fit into the menagerie of lunatics and psychopaths?

I listened for the count, and discovered it was just over four thousand. I had all the thoughts and memories and pictures filed away in my brain; the only thing left to do was to prepare myself to wake up. That was when the work would start for real.

For a moment, I wondered why I was working so hard to remember if I had killed this poor bastard or not. Who Martin Blackston was to me was likely irrelevant, even if I had shot him in the head. If I was guilty, then all the working out, the mental transformation, and the visits from dream women was for nothing. All I was doing was trying to become something I wasn't, which was a decent human being. Killing someone like the doctor said I did would make me the worst kind of human being, and I would deserver whatever punishment could be dumped on me. Hell, at that point, I would happily assist them.

If, however, I ended up proving myself innocent, that made for the billion dollar question: Who set me up? A better question was why I was set up. Framing me for a crime I didn't commit, especially one so heinous, was just a method of getting me out of the way.

The final question, of course, was even simpler.

How would I make the bastard pay?

Chapter Ten

Five thousand.

In both my head space and in the real world, I was sitting on the floor with my legs crossed. Outside my brain I could not be seen, as the mat that was the poor excuse for my bed was on the ground against the wall farthest from the door. The pencil-mark thin line of light at the bottom of the heavy iron door was the only break in the solid darkness around me. The lack of sound and echo was almost physical, with my breath being the loudest thing in the room. My fingers traced the floor, feeling the rough concrete outside the mat's pitiful range. I listened carefully to the way my flesh traveled over the material, the sensation almost like reading Braille written by a drugged-out orangutan. The sound of my fingers was swallowed up by the dark, the sensation seeming more transferred through my arm than through the air.

My back was to the wall, but I couldn't feel the stone getting any warmer from my body heat. I shivered, scratching my shoulders through the material of my sweatshirt. The sensation was biting cold, the wall very nearly like dry ice, feeling like it was going to peel not only the clothing covering my back, but several layers of skin as well if I didn't keep moving enough to keep from getting stuck. It was a burning cold, the kind of cold one expected in the bowels of winter either at the top or bottom of the glove, always moving, always trying to keep myself from getting stuck. Staying still would just get me sick.

I knew I must have looked the fool, rocking back and forth to warm myself and keep myself mobile, but I doubted I could have cared less. I was the only one in the Hole, at least my little part of it, and I really didn't give a sweet shit what anyone thought looking at me. Considering it was so dark I couldn't even see my fingers touching my nose, I knew my appearance mattered not a bit. If I could be seen, I suspected whoever saw me would wonder at the wild hair, the glazed over eyes. They would see a small scrape on my forehead, where I had bumped a wall tracing the interior of my cell. It bled only slightly; the cold was staunching the blood flow, otherwise I'd be bleeding like a stuck pic. They would, however, not see me reacting to anything. I was in a world of my own doing, and there was nothing except myself or a world-shattering even that would bring me out of this trance. The trance was a self-induced state, some resurfacing skill brought up from the bowels of my moth-eaten memory. They would also notice my rocking went in metronomic rhythm, counting off a multitude of things as well as keeping my back from freezing to the wall. Each rock was one second. Thirty complete rocks was one minute, three hundred was ten minutes, and so on.

Keeping time was mostly just to realize when I would be dragged out for my fight with Ira. Though I couldn't hear him in any of the cells nearby, I knew he was there. Likely he had heard I was stuck in his own backyard, and was salivating at the idea of teaching me a lesson there and then. I wasn't too concerned about the idea; after all, Saturday was well over a day away. If Ira stayed true to form, I had nothing to fear from him until we stepped into battle.

Mentally, I laughed. There I was, in the bowels of an insane asylum, being a human metronome. Trapped behind a solid iron door, in a room that could be called charitably a sensory deprivation chamber, formulating multiple strings of thought in regards to a murder case where I was the sole suspect. Of course, I couldn't forget the other inmates of the place, who were bad, but the orderlies, who either made my skin crawl or tried to help me.

All that, and I was planning a strategy against a bloodthirsty killing machine who likely sat no more than a few yards away, plotting to pull my innards out to show the whole world what I was made of. No one could say I wasn't an industrious son of a bitch.

Ira was, oddly, the lowest priority on my mental scale. As I began a new count in my head, this time counting up for how long my brain was clear, I started visualizing the filing cabinets. They were tall, metal things, painted a dark green, battered by hands hitting them and the drawers being slammed closed. The cabinets had the feel of old friends, like I always had them, and they were part of my life. Déjà vu struck me hard, making the room around me sway before I got myself back under control. The self-taught crash course in diving into my own head was amateur hour, since there was no one to help me. If I wanted to do something, I had to do it myself.

From the cabinets came the files and their contents. Pictures and words flew out from the drawers in the form of manila folders, like something out of a cop drama show. The flying was more fanciful than I would have liked, but I chalked it up to the remnants of drugs in my system. The last thing I wanted was some mumbo-jumbo magical crap going bibbidi-bobbidi-boo and making me think I had some super powers thanks to a scar on my head. I wanted no more delusions.

It was at that point I discovered just how cynical I was getting, scar or no scar.

The fog in my skull dissipated, allowing me to expand the room in my mind to something more workable. I didn't need the meat part of me to bother with stupid details like breathing and other autonomic responses. I mean, who needs that kind of distraction? Time seemed to flow slower outside my head, which was fine by me; I needed every edge I could get. The metronome in my head started slowing, stretching out the space between ticks of the clock. My heartrate dropped down to a steady sixty beats per minute. My breaths were spaced out evenly. The rocking ceased as I internalized everything that made me who I was. I needed to dive into my brain and work out all the details, of the killing and exactly who the hell I was. The latter seemed to be where my mind was going for the moment.

The amount of knowledge that was filling my head was frightening but useful. A week ago, I barely knew how to stand without cringing at the faintest sound. I would miss screamingly obvious clues for anything and everything under the sun. Someone could shout a simple three word sentence into my ear with an air horn and I'd still miss what they were talking about.

Skills and abilities poured over my brain, filling in the holes I knew were there, and others I had no clue existed. As a great example, the turning in on myself. I mean, I had done it before, obviously, with my dreaming, but not with this level of expertise and not consciously. With what was coming alive in me, I could go anywhere I wanted, create anything I needed, without any fuss. That made things easier to analyze, and that was what I needed. I took a figurative deep breath and began.

I cleared out everything from view except the table, the cabinets, and the files. Those would stay. The rest vanished from view, allowing me a blank slate to create what I needed the crime scene.

An alleyway in the city of Newport News, specifically the downtown part. It wasn't the nicest place in the world, but then most places weren't. My mind brought up the pictures, and I painted the landscape. Dark alley, near midnight. Brick walls on both sides. The red of the bricks was faded to a dusty brown after years of neglect and broken promises of rebuilding. The walls went up several floors, but I didn't see where they finished. They weren't part of the scene. Rain dripped down from above, coating everything in condensation. Droplets ran down the walls, like beads of sweat when they got too big to just hang there..

The dumpster overflowing with garbage. Remnants of meals and bags of waste open to the world, their stench clogging my throat, making it hard to breathe. Lights from above, dingy grey from age and neglect, bathing the stone ground in weak illumination. There was some light coming from the windows; not a lot, but enough to bring out more details. The sounds of television shows going on from the seedy apartments above and around me. I could hear them all, most tuned to gibberish. Cars drove by the mouth of the alley, blocked from seeing the location of the killer and his victim behind the dumpster. It was a perfect little tableau for a murder: hidden, private, with no chance for anyone interrupting. There were three cigarette butts to the left of the victim. Menthols, and all the same brand. One of them still smoldered, having just been finished by the dead man kneeling. It had been a last request before dying, and made sense in a macabre way. It wasn't smoking that would kill him.

From the looks of things, that honor was mine.

There was other detritus on the ground: moldering cardboard, ruined newspaper, a used condom from one of the johns who frequented the area, trolling for a piece of ass. This alleyway was its own enclosed universe, and nothing that happened here could affect out there. I felt the breeze flowing through the space between buildings take on a more sinister stench that had nothing to do with the refuse container. There was wrongness in the air, and it was focused right where a man knelt in the garbage, his tan slacks wet with dirty water, and a gun to the back of his head.

I looked carefully at the scene I set, and it really looked bad, for my innocence, I mean. I took my place behind Martin Blackston, his head not an inch from the barrel of the pistol I held. The massive gun was a regular Colt Model 1911A, chambered in .45, and was cocked, locked, and ready to rock. There wasn't a tremble in the gun as it held rock-steady near the back of Blackston's head. It was held at almost a forty-five degree angle, water condensing both on my arm and the weapon.

Blackston was sobbing horribly, though that could have just been my imagination and sense of possible guilt. I tightened up the scenario and the sobs tapered off to a sniffle, then nothing. The file said nothing about tears, so I didn't want to add anything that wasn't there in the first place. I could feel the rain on my outstretched arm, see it dripping down Blackston's head into his collar. After a moment's study, I let the scene play out.

The gun bucked in my left hand, kicking like a mule in my palm, the shot hurting my ears in the tight alley. The bullet spat out and into Blackston's skull, sending a spray of blood back onto me and the weapon. I watched the spray of gore splatter against the opposite wall and the victim, the man I killed, fell forward almost majestically. The sound of his corpse hitting the ground was like a piece of uncooked steak smacking a cutting board.

I looked down at the body and then up and around. The window behind me and two stories above opened, the sound of the news filtering down. I knew the newscasters and the format. It was just before the sports, which made it about quarter after eleven on Channel 3. The amorphous face of the witness looked down on me, but I ignored it; the witness wasn't the problem I was having with the whole scenario. I ran the murder again, then twice more.

It was no good. Something was wrong, and I was in the wrong place to see it.

I pulled myself out of the scene, allowing a mannequin to take my place executing Blackston. This time, I pulled up the coroner's report. I was starting to comprehend more of the report, and it was telling me there was evidence of back spatter from the gunshot wound. I added that in to the next run, this time staying out and watching as much as a dispassionate observer as I could. Still, I winced when the gun went off, erasing most of Blackston's face as the bullet exited the skull just below the nose, through the beard's well-trimmed moustache.

Watching my stand-in closely, I saw it put the gun behind it in its jeans, dragging the barrel across the white t-shirt on its way. It then made a hasty retreat down the other end of the alley, leaving Martin Blackston to leak out his brains and blood onto the uncaring stone ground. I squatted down to look at Blackston's head and saw the stippling of gunpowder around the wound. I shook my head in disgust. At least the kill had been relatively quick. That much damage would have been instantly fatal.

The muck that was getting watered down by nature was disgusting to say the least. The new detachment I felt was welcome, keeping me from throwing up what little I had on my stomach. I chuckled in spite of myself, remembering this was all in my head, and puking in my brain wasn't exactly how things happen.

"Would have made one hell of a mess if this was real, though," I mused aloud, the words flat and not echoing, since I wasn't really in a brick-lined alleyway.

Anyone who has been thinking hard on any complex problem has been at the point of tearing their ears off because something has been eluding them, dancing at the edge of their thoughts screaming neener-neener, and generally being an asshole and not coming forth to explain just exactly what it all meant. They'll be wracking their brains for hours, days, even weeks, trying to get those two pieces of a puzzle to fit together, and they just can't, since there's one connector-piece missing, and it was in the box just a minute ago, and they saw the son of a bitch, and by all they held dear, they would find it or die trying.

Suddenly, that missing bastard of a piece appears, and it all makes sense. There may not be hosannas of angels singing, or a double-rainbow popping out of the clouds, but there is that moment of clarity when it all fits together. That's when they don't feel like the biggest dumbest people on the face of the earth for saying there was a piece that was supposed to go there. They can say the damned thing is *right there*, and don't you feel like a dumbass for not finding it in the first place.

Four words: one hell of a mess.

Mother fucker. I really was looking in the wrong place.

I erased the scene around me, keeping the table and files, along with the attendant file cabinets. There was a new area to create, but this one was easier to detail: Dirty building in the middle of a forested area. Dirt path leading up to it. Still Newport News, and I knew this as the Hunting Ground near Fort Eustis. It was the visual opposite of the alley, teeming with nature instead of urban sprawl, but I could feel the wrongness of the place. Bad things had happened here as well, and it involved me and in some way Blackston, but not the way the files said.

My stunt double was pinned to the wall of the building by several sets of headlights, all of them high-powered and burning the darkness away. I froze the scene I created from a picture lifted from a dashboard camera. It was easy to get rid of the words describing date and time and identification of the officer, though the name in the corner, Elder, gave me pause. I pushed the curiosity down; I could chase minor details like that later. For the moment, I needed everything in this photo to appear exactly as it did that night, not more than forty minutes after a bullet crashed through the skull of an innocent man.

I entered the scene, and it was surreal. The angle of the picture was off, causing me a bit of vertigo as I walked to myself.

That was creepy, so I made the face someone else.

I corrected the angle, flattening out the scene and looking carefully at the guy. He had his hands up, ready to surrender to the police who came to take him away. I had the scene paused, so it was easy for me to get behind my doppelganger. The gun wasn't there, but in the left hand, pointed at the sky. It looked different, as well, but I left that alone for the moment. I wondered how far I could push this simulation in my head, then figured out I didn't have to do anything of the sort.

Kicking myself for not figuring it out earlier, I noticed what my stand-in was wearing. Cheap Blue jeans , and a t-shirt, the kind that go on under button-down shirts. A white one, the tag sticking up from the neck. A plain white t-shirt.

A plain white spotless t-shirt, to be exact.

I brought the file over and read aloud the words I had memorized carefully. "Suspect wearing jeans and white t-shirt, same as witness from alley described." A slow warm smile formed on my face.

Not everyone can be a master of forensics. Hell, even those who do it for years on end run into new things on occasion, and the television shows rarely got all the details right. This, however, was simple biological physics. It's easy to demonstrate. Take a small puddle of paint, put it on the wall. Since this is an example, the paint stays in a small puddle and doesn't drip down to the floor. Now, whack it with a hammer as hard as you can, then pull the hammer away immediately. See the paint that follows the hammer back and gets all over your nice clean clothes? That, in quick and dirty fashion, is back spatter. Unfortunately, back spatter doesn't usually have enough force to travel over two feet with any real success, the laws of physics being what they were.

It does, however, have enough to spatter blood an inch or three to the barrel of the gun used to create it.

In the alley, I saw the mannequin brush the barrel against the front of his shirt, then down the back as he put the gun back there like some rogue loner cowboy cop that didn't play by the rules. Looking closely, and according to the report and pictures, the shirt was clean in both places, without a drop of blood on it, mine or Blackston's, and it was the same shirt worn during the killing.

Other pieces started clicking. I'm right-handed, and though I could do things with my left hand, it was unlikely I could hold a gun as massive as the Colt with my off hand that easily. The gun itself was wrong, as I had been arrested carrying a Beretta M92F, and could only hold 9mm bullets rather than the .45 caliber rounds of a M1911. There were a couple of other inconsistencies, but I didn't need them. I just needed reasonable doubt, and I had it.

I pushed the scene away again, the table staying. I sat in a chair I conjured and put my face in my hands.

"I didn't do it," I muttered. It felt good to say those words.

"Of course you didn't." As always, from behind me, I heard the woman talk. "Took you long enough to figure out."

"You didn't have drugs pumping through your system, did you?"

There was a light chuckle, then I felt the cold fingers on my neck, kneading the tense muscles there. I let out a slight moan. "You always did like that, didn't you?"

Another piece, this one shadowy and not fully in focus, came into play. "I know you well, don't I?" I felt the nod through her hands as they worked magic on my shoulders. "'Say your name and be free.' Free of what?"

"Everything that's holding you back," she said, and there was deep sadness in her voice. "You've already broken through some of what has been done to you. It's time to go the rest of the way."

I glimpsed some of what she said against the background of the institution. "You're part of what's holding me back."

"I'm a small part, but yes, I'm holding you back." I felt her fingers, still so very cold, tracing a couple of the scars on my scalp. "Oh my Tommy. You can't stay here, and neither can I."

"What do I need to do? Show this to the doctor? He'll let me go?" I shook my head. "He won't, will he."

It wasn't a question, but she answered it anyway. "Of course not. You already know---"

"He's part of what brought me here in the first place," I said along with her. "Son of a bitch."

"That's one way of putting it." She pulled away, my flesh missing the touch even though it was cold. "You're running out of time, though. They'll make their move soon."

That brought my head up. "Who?"

"I can't explain everything, Tommy. You need to figure it out on your own."

I was done with it. "Oh fucking bullshit, lady!" I stood up and started to turn around. A kick to the back of my left knee brought me down. Two frozen hands, one on the back of my neck, the other locked around my wrist, completed the journey of my face to the table with a crunch. The pain was immediate and real, knocking the fight right out of me.

"Are you that ready to say goodbye to me, Tommy?" Her words came through clenched teeth.

Considering how she had me, I considered my answer carefully. "No," I grunted, "but that doesn't mean I'm not getting tired of the runaround."

The pressure lessened as she let me go. "The time is going to come when you know it all, and you'll have to make a choice."

Sudden light flared down from above me. I looked up, the brightness making my eyes water. I didn't catch the implication quickly enough as I felt myself being pulled out of the dream.

Again, her voice faded. "That time is coming. Be ready."

I sighed as I began bringing myself up through the layers of consciousness, the light from above guiding me. "People always have to do the drama crap," I muttered in my head. "Can't be clear and up-front, oh no. Have to be cryptic."

Something was wrong as I woke up. My eyes flew open, showing me a face I had no desire to ever see so close. Milton was holding me by the upper arms, his hot skin burning against mine through my sweatshirt. I could feel my wrists behind my back being bound with some kind of plastic line. Milton's breath was just north of rotten meat, but only just. I gagged and pulled my face away.

"Oh, so now you wake up, huh?" Milton's voice was booming and boisterous, the words echoing in the cell. His statement also allowed that rank halitosis to flow over my face again, which did nothing for my empty stomach.

"Two words, Milty," I sputtered. "Mouth wash. I swear it's not battery acid."

The ziptie around my wrists tightened with a quick pull. I did what I could to keep circulation going, but it was close. "Smart guy with a smart mouth, eh?" Dante said from behind me. "Think you can figure things out by yourself?"

For a wild second, I thought they had been poking around in my head, or I had said something while doing the mental CSI thing. It hit me what they meant: I had left stuff under my mattress in my room, namely pieces of my file I had stolen. I mentally kicked myself for being so stupid. "What's it to you if I know the truth?"

"Means we'll be out of a job, Statford," Milton spat, saliva landing on my cheek and shirt. My flesh crawled where it landed. "We have to fix things."

"Yeah," Dante echoed. "We gotta make sure you don't go nowhere, so we're having your little fight early."

Shit.

"Don't worry, though, Statford," Milton said. "It'll technically be Saturday. Somewhere. Maybe."

"I got him trussed up like a pig for a roast, Milton."

"Good, Dante. Let's get him to the basement. He has adoring fans waiting for him."

"It's about time we got this done. Our patron has become impatient."

The two ogres partly carried and mostly dragged me through the now-bright hallways, down the stairs, and to the basement. The whole time, my brain is screaming that this was wrong, this was against the plan, and this is not supposed to happen. I had absolutely no idea what this plan was, but I couldn't disagree; I doubted when I was born that my destiny was to get into a fistfight with a lunatic at the behest of two corrupt orderlies.

Something was very wrong indeed, and I was about to find out just how wrong.

Chapter Eleven

One of my favorite movies when I was growing up would surprise people. In fact, it surprised me, since it was a sequel, and as a general rule, sequels are usually little more than rehashes of the original and rather crappy rehashes at that. They never add anything really important to the story, and for the most part were just outright cashgrabs for all concerned. Even the actors who were in it thought it sucked, and people end up disavowing even knowing the movie exists, like the baby pictures of you in your birthday suit eating your chocolate birthday cake and basically wearing it.

No, I don't have any pictures like that, and no, you can't see them.

Then there was *Mad Max Beyond Thunderdome*, starring Mel Gibson and Tina Turner. Just an all-around fun movie that expands the world of Mad Max and is one of the best and most-loved post-apocalyptic films out there. There was a chemistry and a formula that really just worked. The soundtrack was fantastic, too, and I don't care how old Tina Turner gets, she can still work those lungs a thousand times better than most of these modern day flash in the pan singers.

One of the best scenes of the movie was, of course, Thunderdome. Everyone who has seen or even heard about the movie knows how it goes. "Two men enter, one man leaves." Darwinism at its finest and most pure. In the film, it was essentially a fight to the death between Max and some huge monster of a man, and Max isn't supposed to survive.

As I was thrust into the basement arena, my hands still bound behind me, I began to wonder just when someone would start singing that we don't need another hero.

The place wasn't much changed, other than the extra lighting from more lamps and better-wattage bulbs in the hanging lights that still swung back and forth in the slight breeze. The ceiling was about ten feet above me, which seemed rather excessive until I remembered the boiler was somewhere in this cavernous place. The pipes snaked everywhere, forming natural walls and obstructions of metal. Knobs and spigots stuck out at various places on the pipes, looking dangerous and quite painful if they made contact. My clothes, not too clean anyway, were sticking to me from the humidity, and it was tough to pull the thick air into my lungs. The floor was covered in dirt and footprints, with what looked like hundreds of different patterns of soles tangled together. It looked like the area I was to fight was about thirty feet across and mostly a regular square. There were several entrances and exits formed by the pipes, but what looked like hot steam blasted out at irregular intervals. Think *A Nightmare on Elm Street* meets *Fight Club*, and that's where I was stuck.

I was pushed to the ground and I lost my breath from hitting the floor. The ziptie around my wrists dug into the flesh, and I could feel blood starting to flow. I scrambled to my feet, trying to get my bearings. Since I was in the arena, that meant Ira was either on his way or already there, and I still had my hands tied behind my back. The knowledge was still filling in the holes of my moth-eaten brain, but none of it had a cure for a gigantic psychotic homicidal murder machine with my name on his fists. Most of the ideas I was having included running, and by "most", I mean "every single one."

"So this is fair," I shouted, my voice echoing off the brass and concrete. "You think you could cut me loose?"

From the darkness, Dante answered. "Sorry, Tommy Boy. Can't let you get free. Boss's orders."

This was bad. What was worse, I could hear others in the darkness, watching this whole affair take shape. They were chanting Ira's name, like something out of a gladiator film. It started low, the gradually lifted in volume until it sounded like there were thousands of people screaming his name. I was starting to get the feeling I was the definite underdog in this matchup.

Looking around, I saw a small pipe that looked to be venting steam. I knew it was going to hurt, but I was running out of both time and options. I made my way over to the pipe and, after a couple of burns, got the plastic on the scalding metal. I felt it start to stretch and deform slightly under the heat, and I pulled my wrists apart all the more. The thin plastic cut deeper into my wrists, but I could feel it get looser.

Then, Ira made his appearance.

He walked in. No, it was more like he strode in, rolling on legs as big around as tree trunks. It almost felt like the ground quaked as he made his way through the entrance of pipes and to the center of the ring. There was no doubt here who was master of this domain, and Ira had no compunction of being shy about it. His skin glistened with sweat and light as he stood shirtless, rotating in place to accept and absorb all the adulation he was getting. The glow in his eyes was orange like the coils on a stove they were dead to all but anger and hatred. Ira's arms looked to have gotten bigger, the muscles writhing like snakes underneath his flesh as he flexed for the audience.

And then he turned to look at me.

And he smiled.

That was almost the moment I decided I was well and truly screwed.

"They said I could have you early, meat," Ira bellowed. "Rules said I couldn't have you until tomorrow, but hey, fuck the rules. Don't see why you're so damn special anyway." His smile grew bigger and he licked his lips. "Supper time."

That, folks, was the moment I knew I wasn't screwed.

I was fucked.

Ira roared as he came at me, covering the fifteen feet in only a pair of seconds. I saw the move coming and dropped down and to my left, rolling away to my feet. I could feel my left shoulder give a bit more than it should when I completed the roll, and I hissed in pain. The ziptie was still just tight enough to keep my hands tied. I looked up to see Ira pounding the wall of pipes, red welts on his face and arms where they touched the hot metal. His noises were pure anger, not pain.

Taking the chance, I got down on my back and pulled my legs over my wrists, the usual method of getting bound hands in front. I was lucky enough to get my feet untangled from my wrists, but not without pulling my left shoulder even more. The creaking from the joint was worrying, but I figured I was okay for the moment.

That moment ended as Ira fetched a kick against that same shoulder. Blinding pain rolled through me as I tumbled and smashed into the hot metal wall. I screamed as the pipes left long lines of sheer agony on my back through my shirt. To add injury to injury, I heard the grating in my shoulder and knew it had been popped right out of socket.

The only good news of the whole thing was I had slipped out of the ziptie, which hung pointlessly from my newly nearly-useless left wrist. So that was something going for me, which was nice.

I got to my feet. I was shaky, but I was vertical. I took a quick mental tally of places that didn't hurt on me, and the best I could do were my eyebrows, and they were getting a little singed. Ira took a swing at me. No form, no style. Just a haymaker that would knock my skull into the next area code. Ducking it was easy, which it was supposed to be, as his left fist spun around on the followup, catching me across the jaw. It wasn't as hard a hit as the right hand would have been, but that was like saying you were lucky to be hit by a sedan instead of a bus.

Spinning out of control, I fell to the ground again, this time on my dislocated shoulder. The pain was galvanizing, clearing my head for a brief moment. I looked to see Ira barreling down on me at full speed. When he got to me, he stopped and lifted a foot the size of a loaf of bread wrapped in a leather boot. I saw his other leg and did the only thing I could do: I kicked his kneecap out of socket.

The effect was immediate. A yell of rage and pain filled the area, and I took advantage of it. I scissored his leg between my feet and twisted my entire body, sending him to the ground on his back. A storm of dirt and dust flew up on his impact, and I jumped on top of him, my right fist pumping into his face again and again. Straight shots, back hands, hooks. I hit him with everything I had, and I thought I was doing okay, considering all the blood that began flowing from his nose and lips.

Therefore, it was a surprise when Ira grabbed my fist in one of his enormous hands and squeezed. With his other hand, he grabbed me by the throat. Air started becoming a precious commodity in my lungs as he rolled the both of us over until our positions were reversed. I stared up into the face of hate.

"That was a good effort, meat," Ira said, his words muffled by the mangled state of his mouth. "Too bad it was all against you from the start." He released my hand and hit me right in the forehead as hard as he could.

When I was a kid, televisions used to need a whack on the side to get working again. Sometimes, they needed just a small tap to work properly. Other times, it took several thumps in various places, like those games where the little ball needs to go into the hole. Then, there's the time when it takes something akin to a thwack with a frozen trout to get the damned thing to show the latest reruns.

This was one of those times.

My head fell back loosely as my body went limp in Ira's hands. I twitched a little, but that was all I did, at least on the outside. In my head, what had been a trickle became a spray, then a stream, and finally a flood of memories, telling me everything, showing me everything. Ira let me drop to the dingy floor, and I let myself fall, hearing him call out to his admirers. I was overcome with thoughts, feelings, and emotions from other days, and other times. I saw people. People I knew and loved and hated and would die for and would live for. Places flowed by, the locations matching places in my dreams. Everything started making sense as I felt life, *my* life, come back to where it belonged.

I remembered.

I remembered everything.

I got to my feet a bit unsteady, but that was fine; it was better than staying on the ground. Ira's back was to me, but that wouldn't last long. Taking my dangling left arm in my right hand, I knew what I had to do. With gritted teeth and a count of one, I shoved my arm hard back into socket. The pain was immediate and immense, but I grabbed onto it and used that pain to finish the job. It only took a second of grinding and pushing, but I got my arm back where it was supposed to be. I let out a gasp before taking a deep breath to steady myself.

Apparently, Ira got wind that I was standing up after his supposed knockout punch. He turned around to face me, regarding me with a curious look I had never seen on him before. I filed it away in my head, not giving a damn whether it was amazement or fear on his face. With a beckoning gesture, I let a cold smile form on my lips. Ira answered it with a bellow and charged.

I knew what I was dealing with, and my brain picked out the nerve clusters and pain centers that had been taught to me by my dear mother. They showed up as bright green spots in my vision, targets for achieving maximum damage with little effort.

There were three places to strike first: one under the left arm, another just under the sternum, and a third in the throat. The hit to the artery under the left arm would disorient, the strike to the xyphoid process would cause loss of breath, and the throat punch would block off any incoming air. The good thing was, I only needed to use one hand to do them all.

As Ira ran at me, I moved like liquid to my right and struck right into his undefended left armpit with my right fist. The impact spun him to face me, letting my left hand land a solid shot to just under his sternum. Before he could vomit anything, I flattened my right hand into a blade and chopped at his larynx, cutting off the flow of anything in either direction. It was as simple as one-two-three, and he crashed into the metal walls, sliding to the floor in a heap. I smelled the burning flesh against the metal pipes and found I really did not care. His body was just a disguise, and a little pain was just what this bastard deserved.

Even with my left shoulder throbbing from the use and abuse, I felt good. Better, actually, than I had in what felt like years. My head rang a little from Ira's punch, but the blow had paradoxically cleared out the cobwebs that were blocking my thoughts. I knew what I was facing, and what I had been locked up with for I had no idea how long. Things could just never be simple.

Ira's head turned toward me, and I saw what had happened when he tumbled. The metal had burned away most of his face down to the bone, the heat cauterizing the wounds as they were made. His cheek was nearly flayed away completely, the muscles and tendons of his jaw flexing and tensing as he tried to get his wind back and say something to me. The horrors had been visited on the rest of his body as well, with two nozzles embedding into his right arm, and another pipe stabbing into his side. As he stood, the cooked-in metal tore away his flesh, letting new, fresh blood flow down his side. I almost felt pity, but I knew it would never be returned. Ira never had and never would feel pity, or any other emotion for that matter.

He stood before me, swaying, bleeding from several of his wounds, and I nodded at him. It was time to finish it. His right arm all but useless, Ira led with his left fist, which I helped to flow past me, guiding it my right while twisting in close. My right elbow came up and hit in his already wounded right cheek, the joint digging into the gaping hole. Fresh blood squirted out from the mangled jaw, covering my tattered sleeve, and I followed up with a vicious knee to the balls, knocking Ira back a few inches. I punched him again with both hands, making combinations into his stomach and face. The hits were measured for maximum damage, most of the blows going into the gaping wounds left by the pipes. Ira tried to block, but he had all he could do just to keep standing. One good right cross closed his left eye, and a left caused his already damaged nose to explode in his face. I gripped both hands behind his neck and pulled his face down hard onto my knee, following up with an elbow under his jaw, which shattered most of his front teeth. Inch by inch, I forced him back. I had him done and beaten, even though he would not go down, and I knew there was only one way to end this.

I kicked him in the stomach as hard as I could. It was an easy target, as he just swayed in place. My foot struck solidly, propelling Ira back against the burning nozzles and spigots, impaling him on the metal. One pipe went all the way through his chest, and he grabbed it, trying to pull himself off it. I just shook my head at how he just would not give up. I had little to worry about even if he managed to pull himself off; the resulting destruction of his form would render him pretty much useless.

As Ira pulled at the pipe sticking out of him, I felt a bit worried. Sure, my skills were back, but it was never that easy. With a bruiser the size of Ira, I was usually guaranteed at least three broken bones, a torn ligament, and a baker's dozen concussions. Sure, my shoulder was dislocated, and threatened to swing uselessly in the breeze if I let it, but all things considered, I got off light. That never happened.

When Ira finally went limp, I spared him no further thought as I walked to the entrance he used at the beginning of the fight. My mind was still full of whirling thoughts, but I had a good idea where to start to look for answers. Time to visit the good doctor, and maybe get in a few bits of revenge there.

That was s when I found out why the fight had been so easy.

My feet got me about three steps before I felt two pinpricks in my back. High voltage coursed through my body, arching my back and paralyzing me to the ground. I couldn't even scream as I lay there, electricity still pouring through my nerves. As I twitched on the floor, the flow of juice finally stopped. My muscles twitched in remembrance of the painful stimulation, and I tried getting back up. I might as well have tried lifting a car with my tongue.

"Oh, you shouldn't have done that," Milton said. I looked up at him and saw the taser in his hand. The wires were still connected to the weapon, and I hated him for getting in my way.

"He's right. You shouldn't have done that," Dante echoed. "Our patron will be most upset."

"Not if we do what we should have done months ago." Milton's eyes lit up.

"It should work. We just have to put him to sleep." Dante pulled out a syringe with a blue fluid in it.

I tried pulling away but couldn't. The stick of the needle wasn't gentle at all, and whatever they shot me with was cold, colder than ice, though I shouldn't have been surprised. I had an idea where I was, and if I was right, it was only going to get colder when I got out. First, though, I had to get out, and I doubted Dante and Milton would be on board with that. As my eyes drooped closed, I promised myself I would be persuasive.

As persuasive as I could.

Chapter Twelve

I should have known I would end up here.

I had returned to whatever the mystics called that place your
mind goes when it was decidedly out to lunch. This time, though, it
was a blank space, with nothing visible beneath my feet, and nothing
to see anywhere I looked. The ground was solid beneath my Chuck
Taylor hightops, which was fine. I drew my coat around me, the
sound of the black leather's creaking like a long lost friend. The
jeans and shirt were my usual fare, black and grey respectively. They
felt good on me, like I had never worn anything else.

I should have guessed that whoever put me in the institution
would blank my memory to keep me pliant and docile. If I had full
use of my faculties, I wouldn't have been a complete waste of space
since waking up in the chair. The dreams were my subconscious
trying to bring me back from an abyss. Mr. Sonofabitch was the
survivor part of my mind, a real nasty piece of work who would cut
whatever throat it took to make it. The bolt of lightning must have
reunited us. That explained the changes in attitude after that first
dream; I was no longer just Casper Milquetoast, but an amalgam of

Sonofabitch and Casper. I was almost whole again, but I needed to let something go.

I had to let someone go.

I sat down and waited, letting my coat out from under me so I didn't end up sitting on it. Old habits die hard, even when you rediscover them. I didn't have to wait long. From behind me, of course, I heard steps. There was an intake of breath but I held up my hand to silence her. I smiled, and the simple gesture hurt my heart. "Hey, darlin."

"So you finally came all the way back, *gringo*?" The sadness in her voice was a dagger through my mind. "It's about time."

I stood up and turned around in the direction of her voice, keeping my eyes downcast. I wasn't worried about her manhandling me anymore. I just didn't want to see blame and hatred in her eyes. "I'm sorry."

"Sorry for what, Tommy?" She sounded genuinely puzzled. "You didn't do anything wrong."

I was speechless. The silence was heavy, it weighed on me like the weight of the world on Atlas' shoulder, but I couldn't shrug this off. I felt the pain rising, the frustration and angst, welled up inside me until I couldn't take it anymore, "I let you die, babe!" I blurted out as I turned away from her. "It's my fault you're dead. They killed you and it was my fucking fault!"

I felt her chilled fingertips on the back of my neck again, soothing the hot anger in me. "It wasn't your fault, Tommy. None of it was."

"Then why are you dead and I'm alive?" I pulled away from her attempt to quiet the rage burning through my head. "Why did they kill you and leave me alive? What was the point?"

"You're the detective," she said, moving behind me again. Her thumbs went up and down my neck, bringing tension out the same way she did when she was alive. "You'll figure it out."

"Maybe I don't want to." The petulance was back, and this time I knew what it was and didn't give a shit. "Maybe I'm happy with having you here and now, just for a little while longer."

"Oh yeah?" Her lilting laughter played havoc with my emotions, bringing tears to my eyes because it was a sound I was prepared to never hear again. "Running and hiding? That's not my Tommy."

I was weeping openly. "I can't lose you again."

The thumbs stopped abruptly. "Is that what this is all about? Losing me?" This time, she spun me around to face her. I tried keeping my eyes averted. She grabbed my chin to bring my face to hers, and all my fears were realized, and all the agony came rushing back.

With her right hand under my jaw and her left hand on my right shoulder, my dear wife smiled at me. The rush of memory hit me with the force of a nail gun between the eyes. The smile she wore was the same one I saw before she died, her heart cut from her chest and held to the sky in some ritual. She wore a shapeless white dress, covering her from neck to toe. Her arms were bare and as pale as they could be. She smiled at me and I dropped to my knees.

"I should have saved you," I said, over and over. My eyes were squeezed shut and burned from tears flowing down my cheeks. "I was all my fault."

I felt her hands on my shoulders, cold but comforting. "Oh, Tommy, you are such an idiot." She stroked my head, the sensation burning across my scalp. "You couldn't stop it from happening once it started, and you can't save everyone."

Defiance flooded my words. "If I can't even save the people I love, then what the hell is the point?" I wrapped my arms around her midsection, holding her close in a way I never thought I would again. "Fuck them all."

"You remember what you used to tell me when I got pissed off at some *pendejo* getting away with murder or something like that on the job?"

I wanted to shake my head, but that would have been a lie. "'We have to be lucky all the time. They only have to get lucky once,'" I quoted myself. How trite it sounded to me. How ridiculous and dismissive.

"It wasn't dismissive or trite, Tommy." So she could read my mind, too. That was not a shock. I was finding my capacity for accepting such events was growing by leaps and bounds. Besides, she did it while she was alive, too. "It was your way of reminding me that, for all I did, for all I was, I was only human." Her hand stroked my head again. "Just like you."

"What if I want to stay here with you? There's nothing for me out there." I was grasping at straws in an attempt to keep her, and we both knew it.

"You stay, and whoever killed me gets away with it. Besides," she said, "remember those two charming *cabrones* out there? You really think they're going to let you wake up?"

Deep down, I knew she was right, and I hated that she was. Milton and Dante weren't likely to let me keep breathing, let alone wake up. Ira had likely been just a tool to keep their hands clean. Their boss, whoever that was, wanted me out of the way permanently, and moved heaven and earth to make it happen. Those two chuckleheads tried to be clever and it failed. They would take matters into their own hands soon enough.

"Tommy, you're stalling." She lifted my face to hers, bringing me to my feet. "That always means you know I'm right."

"I always thought we had the rest of our lives together, darlin."

"We did, Tommy."

"I thought we had plenty of time, and now we don't have enough." I cupped her face with my hands, her black hair framing her face perfectly, her dark eyes pulling me in as they always did.

Susana traced my ear with her fingers, the way I always remembered. Damn, the memory burned with her caress. "Nothing lasts forever."

"I never told you goodbye because I didn't want you to go." I felt heat on my cheeks from the shame of admitting my weakness.

"I have to go, and you know it, *gringo*." Her hand cradled my cheek, and her smile had sadness in it. "You know what you have to do."

I kissed her gently on the lips. "You're really gone, aren't you?"

"You saw me die, Tommy."

Anger filtered into my voice. "It wasn't supposed to end this way."

A kiss from her, this time. "It never ends the way it's supposed to. It just ends the way it has to."

"I will love you even after the stars burn out, and the gods themselves are no more. You know that, right?"

"I know. Say my name and be free."

I kissed her again, deeply, wishing I could breathe my life into her. It was futile, though, since she was gone, and there was nothing I could do to bring her back. It was time, and I pulled away.

"I'm ready."

"You're a shitty liar, Thomas Statford. You always have been." Tears were in her eyes. "You're not ready."

"I'm as ready as I'll ever be." I turned my back to her, and said six words that crushed the heart from my chest. "Goodbye, Susana. Yours, now and forever."

And when I turned back to look, she was gone.

For a moment, I wanted to take it all back. I didn't want her to go, I didn't want her to leave me. The world could go to hell for all I cared, and Dante and Milton could do whatever they wanted as long as I had one more hour, one more minute with her. The universe could burn as long as I had her.

It didn't matter anymore, though. She was gone. She was no more, not even a phantom voice in my head. I would never see my wife again.

I clenched my fists tightly, Power with a capital P thrumming through my body. I was whole again, body and soul. It was about time I was reunited with myself, so to speak, with all the skills and thoughts and feelings from before I ended up in the prison for spiritual lunatics. And the memories.

Can't forget the memories.

Now, it was time to wake up.

The drugs they had injected me with were magical in nature, which was no surprise, considering where they had me. If I hadn't been so screwed up in the head, I would have recognized where I was and been back home in the time it took to deliver a pizza. Since I didn't know everything about where I was, because I didn't know everything about who and what I was, I didn't have a chance to counter what they put in me at the time. A couple of thoughts, happy and otherwise, a little mental chant a certain six-thousand-year-old spirit taught me, and a push of my newly found and focused will, and I felt the Shackles of Lethe loosen around my conscious mind. Fucking amateurs. Using the Shackles was the equivalent of walking up to someone, shoving a rag in their face and asking if it smelled like chloroform to them. The little tricks I knew took away the rest.

I came to, half-strapped into a chair, much like the one I had first arrived in. This time there was no conductive gel on my temples, nor was my right hand buckled down, likewise my left foot. There was an argument in full swing, and it had all the sounds of a panicked disagreement, or more accurately, a complete fuckass clusterfuck. I kept my eyes open as slits, getting just some idea of where they were and what they were doing.

"We have to be careful!" Milton hissed. "We don't cut right, we'll kill him instead of lobotomizing him!"

"And if we do---"Dante said his voice one of sheer terror. This sounded like a hot topic between the two men. It seemed I was a hot commodity. Always nice to feel wanted.

"If we kill him, the patron will make sure our deaths are long in coming." Milton was arranging several tools on a metal plate to my left, then rearranging them like he didn't know which one went in what location.

"The boss will do more than that, you fool!" Dante was at my right wrist, a strap in his huge hands. He appeared to be in the middle of putting it on when the argument broke out.

Milton jumbled the instruments together with a clang, a bone saw nearly falling to the floor. "We could just tie him down and leave him here." Milton's voice took on an air of hope. "Tie him down and run as far and as fast as we can. Let him be someone else's problem."

I had heard enough. Slipping my right hand out of the barely-closed restraint, I reached for the tray of instruments, grabbing blindly. There were hot slices of pain on the palm of my hand as I gripped something; it felt sharp enough, so I stabbed Dante in the chest. The scalpel went through a rib, cutting flesh and muscle and fat with sickening ease. He let out a scream of pain that mixed well with the crashing and clanging metal tools. I let go of the blade and grabbed Milton, who just stood there with his mouth agape like a fish. With his shirt turning pink from my blood in hand, I brought his head down into my left knee up. The blow missed where I aimed, instead breaking his jaw off at the hinge. Blood gushed from his mouth like water from a statue, dousing both me and Dante, who was trying to get the scalpel out of his chest.

Pushing Milton away towards the glass shelves, I undid the strap over my left wrist, then used both hands to free my right leg. I heard a grunt behind me; Dante had managed to get the blade out and brought it down in the space I was just occupying. The scalpel slipped in his blood-slicked hand, making his fingers slide down the instrument to the sharp end. He screamed again, holding his flayed

fingers in his left hand, trying in vain to stop the blood. I rolled off to

my left, turned, and grabbed Dante's neck in both hands. With no

feeling at all, I let myself drop to the floor, pulling him over the

chair, where he landed chest-first on the embedded handle of the

scalpel. There was a horrid crunch, though whether it was the

instrument, his ribcage, or the chair, I could not care less which.

What I did care was he was not moving for the moment.

The fall had hurt my tailbone, but I pushed the pain away. I

had gotten good at that, thanks to long experience and a bit of very

recent training courtesy of George. I clambered upright, my bare feet

scattering the metal everywhere. There was whimpering to my left,

making my head turn towards it. Against the cabinet was Milton, his

chin askew, his teeth and jawbone sticking through his cheek, tears

of pain coursing down his face, the clear wetness mixing with the

crimson.

When he saw me, he began to scream, unintelligible noises

that were more animal than human. Milton began scooting away

from me on his hands and knees, his shattered jaw a pendulum that

scraped on every movement and moment. I reached down and

picked up another scalpel, this one almost big enough to be a steak knife. Taking aim, I threw it as hard as I could.

My throw was perfect; the blade slicing through his left hand and embedding into the floor. Milton screamed again, pure agony twisted in the sound. He tried to pull the tool out, but it was too deep in the floor for him to even budge it. Blood flowed like water out of the top of his hand, and I didn't care. In fact, I wanted more.

Unfortunately, I didn't have time.

I felt at Dante's neck for a pulse. It was weak, but it was there. I rolled him off the chair and dragged him a few feet from Milton. That son of a bitch I wasn't worried about; anyone capable of making that much noise wasn't going to die anywhere in the near future. Picking up a pair of scissors, I knelt down next to Dante, who seemed to be coming out of whatever fugue he was in. I did the math in my head and shrugged. It would work or it wouldn't. With that decision, I brought the scissors down through Dante's mangled right hand.

The effect was so sudden, I had to jump back quickly. He screamed new life caused by the wound. I paid his curses no mind as I rifled through the cabinets, looking for a few items. It was an older surgical room, but it had all I needed. I started assembling what I wanted, all the while listening to Dante describe in excruciating detail what he would do to me when he got hold of me. I had to hand it to him; he was inventive. All Milton did was moan, though since his jaw was unhinged and sticking out of his face, I could understand his lack of conversation.

When I finished my little science project, I said, "Shut up." For a wonder, they both did. "Here's what's going to happen. I'm going to ask questions. You're going to answer. If I don't like the answers, I'm going to drop this." I held up the beaker of multicolored fluid. "I don't know what it is, or what I put in it, but I'll throw it at the both of you. I don't even think it's stable. It could blow us up. It could blow you both up. It could get us all high as kites. I really don't give a fuck at this point." I bent down and picked up the instrument at my left heel. "That's for after. Now, who wants to tell me who's bright fucking idea it was to put me in this fucking place? Who decided to bring me here?" Neither of them said a word, their eyes locked on the beaker. "Well, if that's how it's going to go…"

"You can't do this!" Dante screamed. "This isn't who you are!"

"I am Thomas Ulysses Statford, Keeper of the Conclave," I spat, "and you have righteously fucked up." I waved the concoction in front of me. "You cannot begin to fathom just how completely fucked you are. You and your patron." I took a bit of one of the leftover solid reagents in a pair of tongs and tossed it on Dante's unwounded hand. The sodium reacted with the moisture in his skin instantly, starting a chemical burn through his hand. Burning pork wafted through the air along with his screams. "Don't tell me what I can't do, you shit."

He threw away the metal quickly, but the damage was done. "I don't know anything!" Dante screamed. Milton shook his head in the negative as well, the bone scraping like nails on a chalkboard. "Please, we didn't mean anything! We weren't going to do anything!"

"Except cut into my brain and maybe just leave me part of the produce aisle if I was lucky," I snarled. These two were nothing more than foot soldiers; they wouldn't know anything of importance. I had wasted enough time with them.

"Since you can't help me, it's time for me to go." I took a piece of string and tied it around the neck of the beaker. Looping it over one of the low-hanging lights, I tied the other end of the string to the far arm of the chair, letting the glass dangle five feet above the varnished hard wood floor. I turned two of the burners on, the flames shooting high and orange. With another pair of scissors, I scored the string, tearing several strands apart. The remaining string began to separate and unravel, slowly but inexorably.

"Tell you boys what: I'm a sporting man," I said, brandishing the bone saw. "You should be able to get free in time to stop it, with a little help and a little bravery." I flung the saw into the floor, where it quivered as the point dug into the wood. "I figure you've got about two minutes or so. Good luck, fuckers." I picked up a small red fire extinguisher. They wouldn't be needing that.

With that, I walked out the door of the operating room, slamming the wood aside as I strode calmly but quickly past room after room. Dante screamed after me, but I was beyond hearing him; His part was done, as was Milton's, and they could both burn.

The deceit that kept me a patient in the asylum was no longer working, and the tangled web of enchantment fell away from the building around me. As I walked past, the walls took on a patina of neglect that only years could cause. The floor, formerly wood that shined with a mellow glow, looked pitted and rotted from bugs and creatures traipsing up and down the hall. Around me, the air became thick with magic and cold, helping to pinpoint exactly where I was. The cold did little more than make my desire for vengeance burn hotter.

After only another set of doors, I found the doctor's office, the entrance made of mistletoe. I grunted at the familial jab and bashed the knob, an ornate thing of brass, off the door with the fire extinguisher. The plate on the door telling me who was inside was in old Norse runes, but I didn't need a translation. I knew exactly who I was dealing with.

With a final blow of the metal container, I sent the door flying open, splintering against the inside wall. I started inside, then stopped as I saw my prey. I hate being dumb, and I hate when I get the answer when it doesn't really matter anymore.

He sat on a throne of black ice, his scepter as tall as he was. Fair skin, coal-black hair, and an impish grin were the first things I saw of him. His clothes were decked out with onyx and emeralds, with some obsidian mixed in for some variety. It should have looked like a mess, but he made it work. Boots of gold went all the way up to his thighs, and gloves of black leather covered his hands. The hand that wasn't holding the scepter cradled a golden goblet filled with some kind of liquid; I couldn't tell what it was from where I stood.

"Thank you for knocking, Thomas," Loki, the Norse god of Deceit said, his tone one of geniality. "I take it Milton and Dante won't be joining us?"

I heard a blood-curdling scream from behind me, then the ear-compressing thump of an explosion. "No." I made sure my tone was as clear and unambiguous as possible. "Explain what happened."

The god sighed heavily and leaned forward. "Yes, Thomas, I think it's time for the truth. I hope you're ready," he said, staring into my face, "because this whole thing is your fault!" Loki slammed the butt of the scepter down and stood. He pointed the globe of the scepter at me, the metal glowing with a bright yellow light. It became difficult to look at, and my eyes watered from the glare.

Godsdammit. Just when I thought things were going right.

Chapter Thirteen

The clock struck midnight. It was time to unmask.

The Norse god of mischief was pissed at me for some reason, and was standing in front of his throne of solid black ice pointing a golden scepter likely of Asgardian origin at my face, or at least the general vicinity of my face. It likely wouldn't matter if he was off by an inch in any direction; it would hurt like a son of a bitch. The scepter was everything a warrior-type would look for in an accessory that doubled as a weapon: fearsome, intimidating, and functional. He was garbed in full Asgardian battle dress, both beautiful to behold and nearly impenetrable to things of a normal nature thanks to the fae enchantments. He stood tall and proud, regarding me with a look of hatred I didn't know I deserved, and to be perfectly honest didn't give a shit.

Meanwhile, I was battered, bruised, and shaved bald. My clothing was in tatters, with my shirt looking like it lost a fight with a flaming rabid wolverine that just drank a gallon of PCP, and my sweatpants that were holding on by a prayer and a memory. My feet were bare; my entire body was covered in a mixture of blood and dirt. Some of that blood was mine, but most of it belonged to the two bastards that got exactly what they deserved. In my hand was a battered fire extinguisher, which was still full. I had a smile on my face, or was it just the look of someone whose give a damn was busted.

We stared at each other for a long minute before I decided to break the silence.

"Put that godsdamned thing down, Loki," I said. "You can't hurt me with it. If you try, I'll make sure that godsdamned thing goes up your ass sideways." I'm nothing if not diplomatic.

"You think merely because you know who you are that you are protected?" Loki's voice took on a different tone and timbre. Gone was the understanding of the kindly doctor. Here was the thundering of a god who was used to having his commands obeyed as law.

"You know the rules; I'm off limits." My warning fell on deaf ears.

"Oh yes," Loki sneered, "the *rules*. Aren't you in for a surprise?" When I said nothing, he continued. "Things have changed since your time on Midgard, Keeper. Many things have changed because of your stupidity."

"What are you talking about, Loki Laufeyson?" I was confused. "My time on Midgard?"

The god stalked toward me, the scepter striking the floor with each step. "Your curse brought down the heavens, just as you wanted, and for two years we waited for you to awaken and give us back what you took!"

My mind flashed back to the ritual, to Susana, to holding her bloody corpse in my arms and screaming at the gods for letting it happen. "That wasn't my fault!" I started forward myself until I was nose to nose with the psycho brother of Thor. "It was your fault that she died! You idiots in the Conclave knew this was going to happen!" I pushed Loki in the chest with the fire extinguisher. He fell back a step, surprised. "You bastards knew she was going to die!" I gave him another shove, harder this time. "You knew those crazy sons of bitches were going to kill her!" I threw the metal can at him, the extinguisher bouncing off harmlessly before I pushed him with all my might. "You knew!"

"We knew nothing!" Loki grabbed me and threw me across the room. I flew in nearly a straight line, striking the wall with my relatively uninjured right shoulder. The plaster had changed to some kind of mossy growth, which broke the impact rather than my shoulder. The god stalked toward me. "One moment we are enjoying a good bout of hunting in the forests, my brother and I actually getting along!" When he reached me, he pulled me up by the front of my shirt, which ripped with agonizing slowness. "Without warning, we are thrown through space and we fall to Midgard, to your pitiful little world!" Loki shook me and my head snapped back and forth like a ragdoll. "I had one of you pathetic little worms touch me in the guise of asking if I was all right." He pushed me back against the mossy wall, and even though it was softer than the stone underneath, my breath still rushed out of me. "The gall! Asking their better if I was all right." He leaned into my face, his eyes slits, his teeth cutting off words like scissors. "His death was quicker than he deserved."

He threw me again, this time at another wall. This time I was better prepared, which simply meant I could choose whether my face or my back hit the moss. I chose my back this time, but the force still sent shocks of pain through my left shoulder. "And now we cannot spend our days in our realms," Loki raved. "Our power is weak, gone to a glimmer of its greatness! You stole our power, Keeper!"

"Bullshit!"

"You brought us down! You made the heavens fall by your words!" Loki brandished the scepter as he moved swiftly towards me. "You---"

I never found out what else I did as I raised the fire extinguisher and unloaded it in his face. The white powder and smoke blew out in an enormous cloud of muck, covering the insane god in noxious foam. I let the whole charge go, trying not to revel in the gasping and the arm-waving he was doing to try and wipe away the chemicals. His formerly black and shiny armor became coated in the stuff, and he coughed, getting it in his mouth. I dodged the scepter as Loki flailed it around, trying to blindly connect with me. The tip caught the stone ceiling, ripping the spear out of his hands, clattering to the floor in front of me.

Not being one to look a gift horse in the mouth, I scooped the metal weapon up, dropping my spent extinguisher to the floor in exchange. The scepter was chilling to the touch, and felt incredibly ancient. I noticed the runes on the shaft, forming words I couldn't decipher. The tangled script went all the way up to the headpiece, which held the sapphire in a grip of steel. It was heavy, but comforting in my two-handed grip.

Loki kept hacking out the chemical mixture from the extinguisher while he tried wiping his eyes clear. I almost felt sorry for him when I saw the tears rolling down his cheeks. Though it was nothing like pepper spray, the stuff that goes in a fire extinguisher can still burn the hell out of the eyes, and hurts like a bastard no matter what. Though I didn't know how the mix tasted, from Loki's reaction, I was getting the idea it definitely wasn't sweet as sugar.

With his eyes finally clear, Loki turned to face me. When he saw that I held his scepter, his face fell into fear for a brief flicker. The look vanished under his trademark smile as he swiped some more of the chemical mixture from his face. "Give it to me, Keeper."

My hands squeezed the metal, the runes digging into my palms. "Why should I?"

As if to a child, Loki chided, "Because you have no idea how to use it properly. Only someone of my skill can wield such a device with any aptitude!"

"Is that right?" I held it tighter. "What can it do?"

"In my hands, it can unleash a bolt of pure force!" Loki scraped more of the stuff off his armor before flinging the white powder to the floor. "It can shatter a giant in a single blast. I can change the weather with it." He looked at me with loathing. "You have no idea how to even power it up, you worthless mortal. You useless quim! You can't even---"

That was when I sent the butt of the scepter into his crotch.

The blow bent him over, pain wheezed from his lips as he staggered. I brought the metal staff up hard into his face with a clang and knocked him onto his back. Puffs of grey smoke billowed from underneath him as he landed. There was an imprint of the runes on the streaked skin of his forehead, and a trickle of blood from his left nostril dribbled down his cheek. He laid there clutching the family jewels, a curious high-pitched noise coming from his throat.

"You were saying?" I smiled, putting the pommel of the scepter squarely between his legs, a few scant inches from what his hands were trying to protect. I took the weapon in both hands as I would a golf club. A grin split my face as I inhaled deeply, filling my lungs with the scent of moss, trees, and flame-retardant chemicals. I drew back the scepter in a way that Tiger Woods would envy and shouted "Fore!" A high reedy whimper sounded from Loki's mouth, his head shaking back and forth, his eyes pleading.

"Let him go, Tommy."

The pommel hit the stone floor inches from Loki's package, sparks flying on contact. The god at my feet gave a cry as he scrambled away from me. "Well, hell, George," I said by way of greeting. "That's going to cost me a stroke." The words were bitter in my mouth, and sounded worse as they passed my lips.

I turned to see George standing in the doorway. His robe was resplendently white to the point of glowing, creating a stark contrast against his mahogany features, the belt around his waist glinted with gold. His shoulders were broader than they were only a couple days prior, and his long, luxurious salt and peppered beard was immaculately shaped. George had aged some, at least physically, looking in his early sixties rather than middle thirties. His tight cap of hair also had silver mixed in with the black, lending an air of wisdom and command to his visage.

"It's all over now, Tommy." George walked farther into the room, his voice quiet as distant thunder over the mountains. "You came back, which is more than anyone thought would happen."

"No thanks to you, George." I shook my head in disgust. Of course He would be here, and it made a lot of sense, considering the other patients of the Twin Friezes Institute. I hated it took so long for me to put things together, but drugs will do that, as well as whatever mystical Norse mojo Loki had whipped up to hide the otherworldliness of the asylum. "Why?"

George chuckled. "To which question? Why did we deceive you? Why did we bring you here?" George walked around Loki's prone form and shook His head. "Why did we allow such horrible things to happen to you?"

I shrugged and said, "Those will do for now."

"We had to make sure you were actually you." George sat in Loki's vacant throne, the ebony frozen water glowing at His touch. "You've no idea just how bad off you were when you were found."

My eyes narrowed. "My wife had just gotten her heart cut out," I said, biting off each word. "I think I know exactly how 'bad off' I was."

George raised an imperious eyebrow. "Not then. After."

"After what?"

"After you brought all of us down from the Conclave. After you brought every god, goddess, and demigod, real or fictional, down to the realm of the mortals." There was no rancor in George's voice, just simple, immutable fact. "After you changed everything."

"I don't even know what I did." I walked over to the wall I had been thrown against, near the door George had walked through. "You know, other than watch my wife bleed out in my arms."

George gave no reaction to my addendum. "So it wasn't intentional, which was what I thought." George steepled his fingers, elbows resting on the arms of the throne. "There were those who thought you did this on purpose, as some way of punishing the Conclave for not leaving you be. They wanted your head on a spit."

"Who?"

"That one right there," George pointed at Loki, "though I think he wasn't serious. Ares, but then, he wants to put everyone's head on a spit. There were a few others, but not as many as you think."

I snorted. "I'm flattered. Why the Cuckoo's Nest treatment?"

"When you were found, you were completely comatose, as if the soul had drained from you." George stood and walked to where I had stood over Loki and looked down at the halfbreed god. "Though our power had been limited, we had enough to create something for you to recuperate. Loki provided the place."

"Niflheim, right?"

George nodded approvingly. "Correct. You know your otherworldly realms."

My eyes rolled in derision. "Comic books, man." I laughed in spite of myself and pointed at Loki, whose gaze was locked on the metal staff. "That guy right there is a heartthrob among the mortals. I'd probably get lynched if anyone saw what I did to him."

"The point is, Tommy," George said, walking past Loki and towards where I leaned against the wall, "we wanted to make sure you would come back as you, not as some kind of mindless beast, or worse, someone who meant to do this to us."

I started to put it together. "Loki is the best you could find at lying, and it's his home turf, which allows him to control what goes in and out."

"It made it easier to provide a recuperative environment."

"What did that make Milton and Dante?"

George nodded, pursing his lips. "Those two were recent arrivals. Since they made it to the place, we thought they were part of some new plan to shock you back to yourself since you were taking so long to come back."

"How long?" Those last two words caught in my head.

"Unfortunately, it seems someone managed to slip them in past excruciatingly meticulous safeguards. That made things more difficult than they had to be, especially given their actions." He continued as if I hadn't spoken.

"How long?"

"They seemed only interested in bullying and harassing the others at first." George looked lost in reminiscence. "They took advantage of poor Ellen. She was a victim to herself and her desires."

"How long was I out?"

George turned his back on me. I was starting to get a bit tired of being ignored. "We all failed to see the signs, though the others didn't really care, nor were they really capable of seeing anything other than their own vices. It should have been obvious what they were doing when they put you against Ira."

I hefted the scepter like a spear and threw it past George and into the throne. The golden metal cracked the ice, launching shards of blackness everywhere. There was a loud peal of thunder as the staff embedded itself deep in the rock. I barely had time to get out of Loki's way as he ran out of the room. Things had gotten too hot for the Norse god, which was lucky for him. I still wanted to bounce his staff of his head five or six more times.

"How. Long." My words were empty of tone, dropping from my mouth like lead.

George took a deep breath, "Two years."

The statement hit me like a truck between the eyes. Things started getting fuzzy around the edges of my vision as I realized the impact of what George said. I fell to one knee and a steel hand seemed to squeeze my stomach. Even though there was no food in me, I threw up anyway, stinging bile leaving an acidic taste.

Supporting myself with my hands, I looked up at George, who stood serenely only a few steps away. He regarded me with a level gaze, and no anger or disappointment. He went on talking as I pulled myself together.

"You almost came back to yourself a few months ago, before Milton and Dante arrived. We nearly had you out of your comatose state, if not for one minor problem."

Memories flashed out of the recesses of my mind. I saw myself strapped down on a chair, Loki in his guise as a doctor working some kind of old Norse mojo on me. "I told you to let me die. I told you all to let me die." I shakily got to my feet. "Why didn't you?"

"Isn't there an old saying about the devil you know being better than the devil you don't?" George shrugged. "It didn't matter; we couldn't let you die. We didn't know what would happen if you did, if your death would banish us to some other realm, or cause us to wink out of existence, or nothing at all."

"So you were afraid of what might happen?" I shook my head in disbelief. "You're gods! You're the ones who can wrap time and space around your nose hairs! Are you telling me you didn't know what would happen, oh omnipotent one?"

"We aren't the gods we used to be, Tommy. Things have changed."

I leaned back against the wall and covered my eyes. "What do I do?"

George laughed. "What you've always done: pull yourself from defeat into the jaws of victory by your own power. Turn despair into hope for yourself and others."

My heart grew cold. "Who set it up?" When George said nothing, I dropped my hands to my sides and repeated myself, adding, "This was not just something someone dreamed up last week. This wasn't a plot someone came up with while in the can reading a shitty fantasy novel. Someone planned this very meticulously."

"We don't know." George was very matter-of-fact. "As I said, we aren't the gods we used to be. It's harder for us to do anything big anymore." He mused. "It's harder for us to do anything anymore, for that matter."

I sighed heavily. "So it's the old-fashioned way. Okay." I walked up to the throne, which was beginning to melt, and pulled out the spear. "Who knows where I am?"

"We kept the circle small. Myself, Loki, Heimdall, and the Seven." George counted them off on his fingers. "There was no desire to let others know your inability to wake up."

"What about my family?" When George said nothing, I bashed the throne with the scepter, knocking a huge section of ice to the floor. "You arrogant bastards," I muttered. "You stupid arrogant bastards!"

"It was considered best that you were unavailable to everyone. There was no desire to bring anyone you were closely involved with into this situation; it was volatile enough as it was. For what it's worth, Tommy, I'm sorry."

"Oh cram your fucking sorry up your formerly all knowning ass," I snarled, heading for the doorway Loki had barreled through. My head was down like a bull's.

George stepped in front of me to block my path. He put a hand on my shoulder. "Where are you going?"

"I'm going home, George. I'm going back to Earth. I'm going to see my family and let them know I'm still alive. I'm going to find the one who started this insanity." I brought my eyes up to meet George's. "And I'm going to annihilate the motherfucker out of existence, and anyone who stands in my way." I looked pointedly at George's hand, which still rested on my shoulder.

He removed his hand and nodded. "It won't be easy."

"It never is."

"Take this." He reached into his robe and pulled out a wooden container the size of a cereal box. "Don't open it until you get back to Earth. Also, you'll want to take a right as soon as you exit the building. That should get you where you need to go."

My hatred of all things godlike softened for a moment. "Thanks."

This time George laughed, a rolling sound that was wind on the water. "Don't thank me. It's payment for taking care of Raziel."

I shook my head. "Nick paid me for that job."

"But I didn't." George smiled. "Just shut up and take it, Keeper. You'll need it."

I grudgingly took the box and walked past George. I eventually found my way down to the entryway of the building I had apparently spent two years of my life. The glamour of the place was gone; it had reverted to a decrepit stone keep, probably one of Loki's old playgrounds. There were dried maroon splotches everywhere, accompanied by ancient bones that looked gnawed upon. Tufts of fur on the ground were covered by layers of dust, some of it swirled up by my passage.

When I reached the front door, I wasted no time in kicking it open. The rotted wood exploded and the rest of the door fell to the ground. Snow fluttered up, the wind twisting it around me as I stared out at the cold wasteland.

It was snow, as far as I could see, but there was no cold. Mists covered the land in eddies and waves of thick soupy fog, obscuring my vision past a hundred yards or so. I spat a curse at the ground at my stupidity; Niflheim was known as the land of mists, so I shouldn't have been surprised that I would be lucky to see more than a few feet in front of me with any clarity.

Watching my step in the mist, I looked around me. The ground was soft with green grass, which struck me as odd with all the snow seeming to hit the windows when I was inside. The sky was hidden from me by the dense fog, as were any nearby trees. The Twin Friezes Institution had been built in the middle of an unremarkable clearing. There was nothing around it of any note, not so much as a bush. It was completely boring. Without further ado, I turned right from the door and started walking, the spear-length scepter in my right hand, the gifted box in my left. As I made my way, I let my brain mull over the revelations.

Two years, and Susana's murder seemed like only a few moments ago. I didn't think George lied to me; he had no reason to do so. There was no point to keeping me in the institution, no point in keeping the wool over my eyes, and no point in lying to me. It even made sense to me, in a sick sort of way. They had no idea what would happen if I just died, and if George was right, they were, for the first time in likely ever, completely out of their element, which was unlimited power. The gods probably weren't faring too well with the situation, which would make for both great comedy and great tragedy, and more the latter than the former.

Gods didn't like being the butt of jokes.

After several minutes of walking, I noticed the way ahead of me brightening in a multitude of hues, filling me with an emotion I had thought dead and buried: Hope. My pace quickened as I headed for what I knew was ahead of me: my ticket home.

I slid to a stop as a horde of dried-out corpses charged from the mists, surrounding me in an instant. I sighed and stood my ground, the staff embedded in the grass. As one of the dead men stepped forward, I took a deep breath.

Sometimes a guy just can't catch a break.

Chapter Fourteen

I'd like to think I'm a reasonable man. In fact, I believe I'm one of the most calm and level-headed people in existence. Considering my occupation and the crowd I ran with, I was more calm than a narcoleptic on a morphine drip. However, I had been pushed, and poked, and prodded, and outright incited to lose my self-control. Not only that, it was encouraged to "bring me back", whatever that meant.

For those thinking that Niflheim, Land of the Mists, is a great place for a vacation, I'll save you the trouble: it isn't. Visibility is terrible, the mists are cold and clammy on exposed skin, and let's not forget the critters that inhabit it and the rest of the Nine Worlds. Giants that eat people, huge crablike things that hide in wait for unwary people, flying things that swoop out of the sky to eat people. The scenery isn't much better, as what can be found in the mists can kill people with a touch or taste, or likely will grab you and kill you. It's like the whole place was designed to cause anguish and make sure you hated every single second of it.

Of course, it could have been worse; it could have been Muspelheim. There's fire there. Lots of fire, along with lava and fire monsters. So yes, it could have been worse.

The only literal bright spot was the gate before me, not fifty yards away. It was, without a doubt, the most intricate edifice I had ever seen. Rubies and emeralds competed with citrines and sapphires for brilliance. It reached up into the sky at least a hundred feet and spanned twice that wide. A huge metal bar crossed the gate, looking almost like iron but not quite. Spires on each side of the gate were also made of the gems, winking and flashing with an internal light. It was beautiful, and it was the gate to the Bifrost, or the Rainbow Bridge, the thing the gods used to go from one world to another.

And there I was, so close yet so far.

I took a deep breath as one of the dead men stepped forward. There were claw marks across his chest, probably from a dragon hunt a few centuries ago. The skin was a lifeless gray, the wounds bloodless. His armor was simple leather with a few plates of hammered steel in strategic places; his chest and stomach were bare. Coming from underneath his metal helmet, were stringy black hairs, his eyes glowing a low bluish-gray. Fur covered his hands and feet, and in his right hand a steel sword, marred and pitted by use and abuse. He trudged forward, no longer moving quickly as the mass had surrounding me. The closer he got to me, the more my skin welted, like steel wool being brushed over it. There was magic here, and gods above and below, I hate magic.

"Mortal," it hissed at me. "Know you where you stand?"

"In front of a walking corpse," I said. "Let me pass."

"Oh?" It seemed surprised by my words. "Think you can order the einherjar about like dogs? We were fighting battles the likes you've never seen long before your many-times great-grandsire was even born!"

I groaned inwardly. The einherjar. It had to be the godsdamned einherjar. Dead warriors carted off to Valhalla to spend eternity eating and drinking and fighting until the day Ragnarok rolled around, and all sorts of bad things happened, not the least of which was the end of the world. The einherjar enjoyed a good fight, and would spend weeks just fighting among themselves to keep their skills up. Because they were dead, they could have almost any appearance, though they usually kept the wounds they received that brought them to the attention of the Valkyrie as a badge of honor.

The Valkyrie were scary and impressive themselves, and though I'd never seen them in person, their reputations as warriors was incredible, as they sometimes had to fight the spirits of those they carted off.

The einherjar, though? Most were valorous warriors who also had a knack for being particularly dangerous fighters. Unfortunately, "valorous" didn't always equate to "nice."

"This is not a fight you want to have," I muttered. My hand gripped the scepter tightly. "I really mean it. Walk away while you can."

"You challenge Skili, son of Skegga?" The corpse threw back his head and laughed, as did the multitude around us. The sound was a mixture of clacking bone and wheezing breath. "You, who barely stand in raiment of cloth? Who carry nothing but a box and a metal staff? What threat do you pose to one who has bested a dragon? Even as I lay dying, I sent my sword, this sword," he held up the weapon, "into its gullet. What makes you think---?"

That was when I struck his head clean off his neck with the scepter, sending it sailing over the crowd. The body stood still for a moment, then began clambering through the mass of dead warriors surrounding us to find its missing part.

Another warrior stepped forward, shield on his back, hand holding a huge double-bladed axe. "You struck Skili, son of Skegga, as he was reciting his death? I challenge you, mortal!" This one was clad in metal plate armor, with chain links and leather between the joints. The plates had engravings of trolls and serpents on them. He pulled off his helmet, which did nothing for his looks; time had eaten away his flesh, leaving only pins of light in his sockets and scraps of tendons on his jaw. "You now face---"

Sir No-Name of No-Importance got a great view of the assembled from above as I sent his skull flying. The body dropped the axe and shield and went after its owner.

"Anyone else feel like playing?" I whirled the staff around in one hand, smiling as I did. "I'm Thomas Statford, Keeper of the Conclave, and fun time is over, you primitive screwheads."

A murmur went over the vast host of warriors at the mention of my name. As one, they stepped away from me, well out of reach of my weapon but not from my anger. I kept my eyes sweeping from right to left, the staff twirling in one hand. One of the einherjar stepped forward, empty hands raised in peace, his weapon in its scabbard.

"Peace, Keeper, we did not know it was you. We beg the forgiveness of one who is touched by the Valkyrie."

"What does that mean?"

"It means you may pass, and we will depart. Good hunting, Keeper." The einherjar dissolved into the mists with a sigh, making me almost wish for a chance to ask more questions.

I laughed at my own ridiculousness. I didn't really care. I just wanted to go home. Questions could wait.

When I approached the gate, I saw a massive form standing in front of it. It was someone I knew held no anger toward me, and most likely protected me in ways I would never know while I was in the institution. He wore his armor now, bright gold and platinum gleaming in the light of the Bifrost gate. His helmet was just as brilliant, and his eyes shone from beneath the decorative antlers on the helm. The spear he carried had a shaft that was as big around as my arm, and the head was three feet of intricately-carved metal sharpened to a razor edge. It had to weigh eighty or ninety pounds, all told, and he held it with no effort at all. He made no effort to impede my approach, and actually waved to me.

"About time you got here, Tommy," Heimdall said, the boisterous voice booming out from the mountain of a man. "Almost thought you got lost."

"Hi, Jaime--- I mean, Heimdall." That would take some getting used to. "It's time for me to go home."

"I imagine it is." Heimdall nodded his head sagely. "The question is, are you ready?"

I looked behind me, over the path I took. Niflheim was not where I needed to be. The place I had spent years was a lie, the reason for my being there pure deception. My only friend in the place was one of my jailers. I had let go the only woman I would ever truly love in the mist-shrouded land. There was nothing left for me here.

"Yeah, I'm ready."

Heimdall put his spear on his shoulder and beckoned me forward. "Usually there's a huge lightshow and chanting and me throwing things around, but I don't think you really care to see it."

I nodded. "You'd be right about that."

"Besides, it's not going to be a smooth ride; no need to drag it out any more than needed." Heimdall opened a small doorway in the gate, just wide enough for me to get through. "Good luck, Tommy."

Taking a deep breath, I walked to the doorway. Looking through was like looking into a kaleidoscope hooked to a ceiling fan. Lights of all colors and brightness flared and spun as I stood at the door. "This will get me home, right?" Heimdall nodded, a smile on his face. "Thank you."

"No need to thank me. I'm just the gate guardian." He flicked a glance at the scepter. "What are you going to do with that?"

I handed it to the god, one of the few good ones I knew, and smiled. "Take care of it for me." Without another word, I leaped through the door between worlds.

How to describe interdimensional travel? To put it bluntly, it sucks. There's a lot of light, a bit of pain, and while you do get where you want to go, it isn't worth the price of admission.

Also, as evidenced by the fact I materialized four feet above a parking lot and landed back-first onto the hard, unyielding ground, it really leaves the state of arrival a lot to be desired.

The wind was knocked out of me on impact, making me gasp trying to get my breath back. Underneath me the stone was wet, and a light mist of rain fell on me from above. I rolled over to my right, my left arm still clutched around the package George had given me. Coughing heavily, I managed to pull in one good breath of air before hacking out another bout of rough coughs. When I could, I pulled in another breath, then another, filling my lungs with good old Midgard night air.

Hampton had never smelled so sweet.

I dragged myself to my feet, which were still bare, and took a look around. Laughter, harsh and choked, came out of me as I saw where I had landed. I may have dragged the gods down from wherever they lived, but it seemed that Someone had a sense of humor.

This was somewhere I knew quite well. I looked over at the crater still marking the place the Black Beauty had gone to meet her maker, engulfed in an explosion. Even two years later, there was still a hell of a hole. My fingers touched the edge of the crater, engulfing me in memories of what had been.

With a sigh, I trudged to the door of my office. The locks looked the same, as did the door itself, which still had my name on it. For a brief moment, I wondered if George had been mistaken, and I hadn't lost two years of my life getting my brain untangled from whatever happened to me, and that I had only dreamed everything that was done.

I wiggled the doorknob and wasn't surprised to find it locked tight. There was a light on inside, but I couldn't see anyone moving around through the window. At the rate I was going, it wouldn't have surprised me if I got picked up for vagrancy by any Dudley Do-Right cops that decided to drive by the place.

Sitting myself on the sidewalk in front of the office door, I decided to check out what George had given to me as a farewell gift. The box itself was unremarkable: wooden, latched with a simple piece of metal, with hidden hinges keeping the form of the container smooth. The craftsmanship would have impressed me if I weren't getting rained on and likely going to suffer pneumonia. The latch flipped open easily, and I opened the box.

"You sneaky sonofabitch," I whispered, unexpected tears of gratitude making my voice hoarse.

On a pillow of silk was my old office key.

I swayed to my feet, still holding both the box and the key. Fatigue that only willpower kept at bay flowed through me, and I opened the door fully. I stumbled forward and was assaulted on all sides by sights and scents and sounds I never thought to experience again. My desk was there, looking as if I had never left it. Papers were piled high in both baskets, along with pens and pencils in cups acting as holders. My chair, a beautiful custom-made leather one my mother got me for a birthday a few years ago was empty. The antique light my sister got me as a housewarming gift was on low, bathing the desk with a warm glow. Pictures of my niece and nephew were visible, at least the frames were, and I knew wedding pictures where there as well. My filing cabinets were there as well, sentinels of times past. The window I had often looked out of while pondering cases showed me Hampton at night, with lights and occasional flashes of lightning in the distance. On the coatrack was my old coat. Not the one Susana had gotten me, but the one I wore before I asked her to marry me.

It was more than just coming home; it was becoming me.

"I am afraid I will have to ask you to leave, sir," a cultured voice said from behind me, where I had kept a couple of chairs, a sofa, and a low table for clients. I saw there was a book with very small words on the pages on the table. "Business hours are over." The voice itself brought tears flowing down my cheeks.

"I don't recall ever setting business hours," I said around sobs. Turning around brought me face to face with my oldest friend. Larrisimus, a six-thousand-year-old spirit, stood before me, dressed in a burgundy smoking jacket and silk trousers. On his feet were slippers that looked way too comfortable to be real. He didn't seem to have changed at all, as his blonde hair was still long and down to his shoulders in waves. The blue eyes were still piercing, and the unlined skin was still perfect.

"I do not think you heard me---" the spirit began, then saw me. "Oh gods. Thomas."

Mustering up all my dignity, even though I was barefoot and wearing rags, I raised my head high. "What's the matter, Larry? You look like you've seen a ghost."

"You are alive?" Violet smoke formed around Larry, solidifying into the armor I saw before.

"Yeah, I am. And I'm really frigging tired."

His right hand holding a silver blade, Larry took a fighting stance. "Prove it."

Oh you have got to be kidding me.

Finding the line of control I had in my head between Larry and me, I pulled it. "Drop the Spirit Warrior act and go sit in my chair for ten minutes. I'm going to lay on the sofa for a bit."

As soon as my words exited my mouth Larry was back in his smoking jacket garb, seated at my desk. I made my way to the sofa and sat, putting the box on the low table next to Larry's book. I sighed; it may have been a secondhand couch, but the damned thing was comfortable.

"It really is you," Larry called out from my desk. "Gods, it really is."

"Yeah, it is," I yawned, swaying in place. One other thing about interdimensional travel: it completely drained you. "I'm taking a nap. Go do whatever you're going to do."

No sooner did I say that than I fell over and for the first time in what felt like forever, I truly slept.

Epilogue

Things really had changed.

The gods really had fallen. I wasn't sure how it was possible, but they certainly were no longer the all-powerful high muckamucks that changed the course of planets in the heavens. On a good day, they might change the batteries on flashlight, at least some of them. Others of the formerly godlike still had some juice. I wasn't quite sure if that was a good or bad thing. For the moment, I didn't care. I had more important things to worry about.

First off, I was no longer the only person who could see and hear Larry. Sure, he could still "go ghost" to everyone else, but now anyone could see him. That would take some getting used to. It did explain how he was able to round up my entire family to surprise me when I woke up.

My mom, Avaline Statford, had been hugging me and hadn't let me go, or even say a word. Every time I tried to move, she squeezed me tighter. I have to admit, it felt good to get a hug from her. Don't ever think that you're ever too old to get a hug from the ones who love you, because you never will be. My own tears had fallen, and like hers, they had been of relief. My niece and nephew were in on the hug as well, both of them crying. My mom's tears were silent, but her words were not. "Don't you ever do that again."

I wanted to tell her I wasn't planning on it, but that could happen later.

I found out that Rika and Renton had taken to "working" out of my office with Larry. I didn't know what they did in my office, and didn't want to know. I did, however, make sure I steam cleaned the entire place before I stayed the night again.

Things were a bit on the hectic side all over the world, as no one had any idea what to do with deities just showing up out of nowhere. Even after time passed, it was still a learning experience for all involved, and everyone was really getting a crash course in how to deal with gods and goddesses and their various forms of action.

Finally, my mom let me go, pulling away with still-wet eyes. There was a wan smile on her face as she took a deep breath. "I knew you were alive. I searched all over for you."

"I know you did, Ma." I felt uncomfortable knowing I had caused her so much heartache from disappearing, even though it wasn't my fault. "No one could have found me."

"Where did you go?"

"I'll tell you later. I have something that needs to be done."

Mom raised her eyebrows and looked at me carefully. "What is it?"

"Someone set it up to kill Susana," I said simply. "I'm going to kill them back."

Thus ends the sixth volume of The Statford Chronicles. Tune in next time for Volume Seven: Best Served Cold, and believe me: it is about to get real. There will also be an anthology coming out featuring this brave new world, with stories by August Grappin, Erika Pryor, and me! I'm very excited about it, and I hope you all enjoy it. Thank you all for reading.